Lost and Found

by Christopher Karam

© 2020

Text copyright © 2019, 2020

All rights reserved. No part of this book may be reproduced in any manner whatsoever without written permission from the author, except in the case of brief quotations in reviews and articles.

This is a work of fiction. Names, characters, places and incidents either are the product of the author's imagination or are used fictitiously. Any resemblance to actual events, locales, organizations, or persons, living or dead, is entirely coincidental and beyond the intent of either the author or the publisher.

For Dave, Kevin and Eddy,
and our childhood memories.

Preface

(1944 Guam)

The soldier stared at his thirty-round, box-style magazine of .45 acp. His Thompson was fully loaded, but he checked it twice, just as his father used to check the front door of their house back in Philly before he went to bed, to make sure it was locked. A nervous habit or such. He was never sure why or when his father adopted that peculiarity. At the time he thought it was unnecessary, but never said anything to him about it. But now he realized. Now he knew.

He slammed the magazine home with his large Irish mitt. The past three days had been nothing but nervous preparation. If it wasn't bad enough that they drilled twice a day, his own inherited nervous tendencies had him second-guessing his own actions.

Now it was for real. To the left and right of him, his brothers lay prone, just as he did. Waiting for the words to set them in motion, like a lit fuse on a firecracker they had often thrown into the sewer grates as kids.

He loved the old neighborhood. The neighborhood where all the houses just seemed to touch each other and run down the street in one long row. The neighborhood where if one friend wasn't home, you just went to the next door down.

He laughed to himself. They were so young once. So full of mischief and wonder. Constantly testing life to see if and when it would push back. Maybe that's why he became a boxer. To see how far he could go, to see how good he really was. Good enough to climb the ranks, winning fight after fight... until the war came. He and several of his friends from that great neighborhood had volunteered to join; to fight for what they felt was right.

First it was Europe, where they helped liberate France, then into Germany and now here... to this island hell. This was different. There were no people coming out into the streets waving flags and shouting praises. There was nothing here but sand, the glaring, hot sun and an enemy so dug in, so bent on never surrendering, it had made him wonder if he should have gone home when he had enough points after the Europe campaign.

The wristwatch he wore looked dwarfed by his large wrist. He had always been a big kid. But that didn't matter now. Death would be the great equalizer. You can't look death in the face and tell him you're bigger or tougher. You can't throw a right hook into his jaw and know under your own power, you can knock him cold. No. Now it was all about the brothers. They supported each other and felt each others' pain. To the left and right they sweated, just like him. Pit stains soaking into their drab green cotton uniforms. Sweat from nothing more than nerves.

He could remember when they would unscrew the hydrant tops down on South Street. They had always waited until the sun was at its peak. Until their shirts were soaked through; until they could stand no more. Then, the relief. Cold water that shot forth with such force, only the biggest kids dared stand in its wake. He was always one of the biggest.

It was his size that got his high school coach to ask about him trying out for the boxing team. He was better than good. He soaked up the instruction like a sponge. Then there were the workouts. The jumping rope, the lifting weights and running into the evening. He missed it so. This was no way to fight. Shooting at someone you never saw before. Someone who most times, was too far away to even see their face.

In the ring it was different. You could see the determination in the guy across the canvas. You could feel him move and strike, and you moved and countered. It was like that for the past three years. But he was no nickel and dimer anymore. He had worked hard to push his way up that ladder. He thought about his last fight. The one that his manager had said would launch him up to a shot at the number two contender out of the Bronx. It was a beauty. He dropped him cold in the fifth.

The neighborhood buzzed with the news. Neighbors waved to him and called out when he walked down the street.

But that was gone now. The war took care of that. He wondered how long this damn war would last and if he'd still have the "stuff" when he got home... if he got home.

He took a sip from his canteen and looked back at his watch, hoping for relief from the heat. Hoping they would be called back.

He looked over to the left and then to the right. He trusted his fellow brothers. They were just as nervous. He knew it. He didn't have to ask. It was just understood. He looked back at the Thompson and remembered to throw back the bolt. "Ok, now it's loaded and chambered."

It was quiet. He listened for anything that would ground his thoughts and give him stability. He had always been gifted with good hearing. He remembered when he could hear his parents talking in the living room on the other end of their apartment. He could remember the company that would come over on Saturday evenings. They would play cards late into the night, with small talk across the table, laughter, taunting, and most of all, the sounds of victory. How he missed those days. He was a lucky one and he knew it. Home was always filled with some kind of laughter and joy.

He waited. Still no sound. His own stomach growled and he remembered the powdered eggs and dry toast he had at daybreak. That's the problem with being a big guy. You always got hungry way before the smaller guys.

He looked to the left and then again to the right. His brothers all still. All waiting. All quiet.

Then a bird... or was it a whistle?

It seemed distant, then it grew louder.
Yes, a whistle. It was followed by shouts.

MOVE! MOVE!
It was the command to move forward. In unison, they all jumped to their feet. The loose sandy ground of the island seemed to move under them, slowing their progress.

TAKE THE HILL!

Again the shout was followed by eager men, trying their best to move forward. He passed several of his brothers as he gained ground. The hill before him was steep. The sun beat down and he searched the hilltop in the distance for any possible target. His finger still on the trigger of his Thompson. It offered little comfort. He heard screams from behind, but he dared not turn around. Forward was the only option. Gun shots around him were deafening. He could only hear his own thoughts.

"Move forward. Keep moving!"

Then he felt it. A blow like someone hit him with a sledge hammer on his hip. The force spun him, like one of the paper pinwheels he had as a kid, that when blown, would spin its colors with such speed and beauty that it was mesmerizing. The sky and clouds were the last things he saw as he hit the ground, dropping his gun and lying prone.

He could taste the warm dirt that had seeped in his mouth when he woke. Was he out seconds or minutes? He could feel pain, but wasn't sure where it came from. He felt nauseous, and couldn't seem to move his right leg. His hand slowly made its way to his hip.

He felt wetness and looked down at his side. It was soaked with blood. He could hear the screams for a medic. All he could do now was wait and pray.

Chapter I

(31 years later)

Glistening sweat flew into the air, as Big Jim Dillon threw a hard, fast jab into the already battered face of his opponent.

Two more quickly found their mark as Jim circled and danced around the ring, as if a rhythm only he knew was playing in his head.

He had trained for several months for this fight, and he had never felt in better shape. Everything was falling into place. He could still hear his manager in his head.

'Watch the left! Keep dancing! Mix up your combinations! Wait for your opportunity!"

Over the last few years, Jim Dillon had made a name for himself that spread well past the boundaries of his lower middle-class urban neighborhood.

It was the middle of the fifth round when the opportunity he was waiting for finally came. Jim threw another hard jab, followed by a right cross and then, his signature left hook, which left his opponent face down on the canvas.

Jim headed back to his corner as the referee started his count. When he hit ten, Jim raised his arms and the crowd cheered his name. "Jimmy! ...Jimmy! ...Jimmy!"

"Jim, what the heck! Are you gonna move or keep daydreaming?"

Jim looked down at the checkerboard, which had a couple of kings in his opponent's favor.

"Where's the fire, Archie? I'm thinkin'."

"Yeah, one of your strong suits," laughed Archie, who was chomping on the bit of his pipe in anticipation of Jim falling into one of his classic double moves.

Jim stared hard at the board. Time had chiseled lines into his brow above his powder blue eyes, and his nose displayed the steep angle synonymous with most boxers. "The ol' gangster nose," Archie would say. Jim sat back in his chair, still staring at the board and ran a small black plastic comb through his grey, thinning hair which he simply wore swept back with no part, then returned it to his front pocket.

"You ever get tired of checkers, Archie?" Jim asked.

"Not when I beat you the way I do."

"No, really. I mean, you ever get tired of the same thing every day? Get up, take my medication, put in my teeth, make sure Jimmy has a lunch and gets on the bus, then breakfast alone, followed by reading the sports section, The Price is Right, then checkers in the park around noon."

Jim stared down at his small pot belly, sighed, and then moved his red piece forward, jumping one of Archie's kings.

"Right back at ya," said Archie, as he responded by jumping three of Jim's remaining four pieces with his other king.

Archie placed his trophies next to the others in two neatly stacked rows.

"Well that about does it!" exclaimed Jim. "I'm pretty much beat."

"You might have a chance," said Archie.

"Ha! yeah, in hell. Don't get your briefs in a bunch; I'll finish. But first answer my question."

"Okay, sometimes it gets a bit old," said Archie. "But I'm not looking' to run a marathon or something. I'm enjoying my old age."

Archie, by comparison had a full head of snowy, white hair. He kept himself in good shape and always thought of himself as hip, regardless of his age.

"Well, I don't mean I'm ready to check out," said Jim. "It's just that I really miss Evelyn and Danny. It doesn't seem like five years. More like yesterday. I've always tried to be tough, ya' know. Especially for Jimmy's sake."

"Hell, you are tough, Jim. Everyone in the neighborhood knows Big Jim Dillon. If you hadn't of gone off to war, you would have been champ. I'm sure of it."

"I'm not talkin' about my opportunities, Archie, they were gone a long time ago. I'm worried about Jimmy's future. He's only nine and has to go through life with no father or mother. Just an old fart who tries to take their place."

Jim reached into his front pocket for his hanky and blew his nose. His front teeth popped loose, but he quickly popped them back in place. "If Evelyn were still alive, it would be easier. Damn cancer! Took my son and then my wife. Shoulda' took me."

"You ever hear from Terri?" asked Archie.

"No. ...and please don't bring up her name."

"Sorry. But I still think you're being a little hard on yourself, Jim. You do your best for Jimmy and that's somethin' to be proud of. That kid really looks up to you."

"Just wish I could do more. Get him outta this damn neighborhood. I tell ya Archie, back in the day, the worst think that could happen to ya, is you accidentally left the top down on your Bel Air and a bird would mess the upholstery. Now you can't leave anything unlocked. Drug dealers on the corners and car thieves walk the streets at night. Was much better in the early forties, ya know?"

Suddenly Archie burst out with laughter.

"What's so funny?" asked Jim. "You think having to lock our doors and windows is some kind of joke?"

"No, that woman on the green just rolled an ankle. In fact I think she broke the heel right off her shoe. Haaa, yup, it's broke. The shoe that is, not her ankle. She's walkin' away."

"How is it you always get to see all the funny stuff?" asked Jim.

"Yeah, remember a few weeks ago when that guy in a business suit stepped in something and was dragging his fancy shoe across the grass? That was a hoot."

"Okay," said Jim. "Tomorrow I get the chair facing the green. Look! This is exactly what I'm talkin' about. See that guy right there? His collar is so wide, it looks like it needs landing gear."

"It's the seventies, Jim. Things are changing. Tell ya what, when we finish the game I'll buy you a hot dog," said Archie with a smile.

"The antique shop doing that well?"

"It's doing okay."

"Thanks, Archie. You're a pal. I'm serious. The best, really."

'Right back at ya', Jim."

"Can I have some of my pieces back, pal?"

"Hell, no. Now make your move."

Chapter II

Jimmy Dillon stared up at the large clock on the wall. The rotation of the second hand would often mesmerize him and sometimes make him daydream.

Mrs. Allen was a fourth grade teacher that should have retired a decade ago. Her glasses sat low on her nose and were attached to a long beaded chain that went around her neck. Her black sweater sat up on the small hunch on her back. In fact, black was her favorite color to wear, as she looked to forever be in mourning. She never smiled and was quick to deal out her brand of justice. She was all too aware of the clock-watchers in her classroom and would often crack a ruler on the chalkboard ledge or loudly on their desks to snap them out of their trance. It never occurred to Mrs. Allen that maybe her teaching skills were somewhat lacking as far as keeping children's attention was concerned.

With the inner city heat of June, there was no escaping the minutes remaining in the school day, as they slowly ticked by.

To the right of Jimmy sat Joseph Paglisi. His classmates called him Little Joe, as he looked a lot like the character from the popular Bonanza TV series. He had short, curly black hair and he even wore the same green denim coat. Jimmy always noticed that Joseph's mom would often pack him the same lunch, which was salami and provolone on white bread. It was a popular trend with moms, to serve up the same sandwich day after day. This curse of repetition was the fault of any kid who exuded joy over any particular lunch meat.

Jimmy was lucky in that area, as his grandpa would often mix up the sandwich rotation, perhaps due to his own memories as a kid.

On the other side of Jimmy sat Michael Savoy. Michael's family must have had stock in Mattel, as he owned just about every Hot Wheels car they came out with, or at least it seemed that way. Michael would show them off on the bus ride to school and at recess, too. He could often be found with his hands in his desk, playing with his miniature toy cars. Of course, he was pretty good at looking up at the right moment as Mrs. Allen would turn away from the chalkboard and face the class. Jimmy could imagine Michael's picture caption in a future year book to read, "Voted most likely to own a car dealership."

Behind Jimmy was Carrie Brown, who was a soft-spoken girl who always dressed nice. But she had a particularly weak stomach, as was the case earlier in the year on two separate occasions.

Once, she got squeamish during a science class when the students were supposed to feed mealworms to their small green geckos. This caused Carrie to freak-out and the gecko jumped off her desk. When Paul Benetti tried to grab the quick green lizard, a chair tipped over and squished the poor creature, which caused Carrie to dry heave repeatedly.

The other incident was more recent when a heatwave came through the state and Carrie had eaten more of her share of hot dogs during lunch period. Feeling uneasy, she raised her hand and timidly asked to go to the bathroom because she felt nauseous. Mrs. Allen, being her usual sensitive self, refused to let Carrie get up from her desk. It wasn't long before the class was thrown into chaos as Carrie let loose the hot dogs she had eaten earlier.

Mrs. Allen had a way of yelling at you that made certain if you weren't already embarrassed enough, you were sure to be traumatized for the remainder of the school year, if not longer. Then came the janitor, Freddy. No one knew Freddy's last name but it was probably something Polish, as he only spoke a few words in English. Everything else he muttered would come out in Polish. He was first on the scene to throw sawdust all over any particular mess. He would then let it sit and soak for a few minutes before sweeping it up, while mumbling some Polish swears under his breath.

Paul Benetti had laughed at the whole hot dog scene, and Mrs. Allen promptly sent him to Mr. Dune's office.

Mr. Dune was a large imposing figure who had a voice like a Sunday afternoon quarterback, but was built more like a defensive end. He would bark out directions, which were always immediately followed.

Only once had Jimmy visited Mr. Dune's office, when he had accidentally thrown a kickball during recess, which bounced off another child's head. The whole incident probably would have gone unnoticed, had the child not immediately started sobbing and then run to the recess teacher demanding swift justice.

Once in Mr. Dune's office, the child in question would be forced to stand in the corner directly between the yellow painted concrete wall and the office mail cubby. If not for counting all the small dimples in the concrete, a child could go mad standing there. If the student didn't know what a right angle was, they surely would know, and not soon forget, after their office session. Off to the side was a glass window, exposing the poor individual to whomever walked by in the hallway. Often the child was exposed to an entire class, as they walked single file past the window to lunch. If Mr. Dune saw the child looking around or clock-watching, he would firmly push their head back into place so their nose was as far forward into the corner as possible, making sure to remind them why they were there in the first place.

Jimmy looked up at the large black clock on the wall. It read 2:20. Only forty more minutes before the bell would ring, signaling freedom. Jimmy would then board the school bus and Gramps would be there to greet him as he stepped off. Then, they would walk together down to the doughnut shop and grab a couple of chocolate frosted doughnuts to enjoy on the walk home.

Jimmy's attention was brought back to the class as Mrs. Allen cracked her ruler down on his desk.

"Did you work the math problem out, Mr. Dillon, or are you clock-watching?" she questioned.

"Uh, I'm still working on it," Jimmy answered.

Suddenly, Joseph Paglisi raised his hand. Jimmy thought for sure Little Joe would get him off the hook by providing the correct answer to the problem Mrs. Allen had scribbled up on the board.

"Yes, Joseph?" she asked in her crackly voice.

"I have to go to the bathroom, Mrs.Allen," Joseph blurted out.

"The whole class was allowed to go to the lavatory after lunch break, Joseph. Now you just sit there and solve the problem," she shot back sternly.

Obviously, Mrs. Allen was unaware of what the real problem was, as Joseph let out a small "toot."

Michael Savoy looked up from his desk and made a face with a squished nose, as the smell of something reminiscent of rotten salami hung in the hot classroom air.

Carrie Brown started to look queasy as Joseph raised his hand again. Mrs. Allen ignored him and shouted out to the class.

"Who has the answer to this math problem?"

Clearly no one was focusing on the math problem, as all attention had now turned toward Joseph, who was sobbing at his desk. Jimmy looked to console him by putting a hand on his shoulder, as a small growing puddle had now formed under Joseph's desk.

"Joseph Paglisi!" shouted Mrs. Allen. "Have you peed in your pants?"

It was obvious to all what had happened, but Mrs. Allen's insensitive question merely made the back of the classroom snicker and hoot at the already embarrassed Joseph."

"You will head directly down to the office!" she scolded.

"No!" Joseph yelled back, with his head down in his folded arms. "I won't!"

"You won't? We'll see about that!" she retorted.

Mrs. Allen walked over to the wall and picked up the phone that hung there. All the kids knew what was coming next, or at least they thought they did. In a matter of just a minute, in stormed Mr. Dune. He looked at Mrs. Allen, and then at poor Joseph, sobbing above his puddle.

"She wouldn't let me go," he said in a meek voice.

Instead of yelling, Mr. Dune gently ushered Joseph up from his desk and asked him to head down to the lavatory. He promised he'd call his mother and ask her to bring a change of clothes for him. Mr. Dune then looked back toward the class in a stern manner. All snickering stopped immediately. The classroom was dead quiet with the exception of Michael, who had viewed the whole fiasco as a good opportunity to play with his toy car lot. Mr. Dune walked over to Michael's desk and looked down at him. Michael must have been lost in some fantasy daydream of car racing splendor, as he didn't seem to notice until it was too late.

"...and what the heck are you doing?" Mr. Dune asked loudly.

Michael looked up in shock with his mouth hung open like a deer staring into oncoming headlights, as no words could possibly spring forth. Then Mr. Dune tipped over his desk in front of him. A myriad of Hot Wheels cars, small rubber balls, a few short pencils with the erasers gnawed off, and several sheets of crinkled, unfinished homework spilled forth from the overturned desk. Mr. Dune then took Michael by the hand and led him up from his chair and directed him to go straight down to his office.

Before leaving the classroom, Mr. Dune shouted at Mrs. Allen.

"The next time a child has to go to the bathroom, you let them go!"

Mrs. Allen looked shocked and said nothing. It seemed like sweet justice when Mrs. Allen couldn't even muster a reply to the hulking principal. A few smiles appeared on children's faces as Mr. Dune delivered his parting words toward Mrs. Allen before walking out.

"Call Freddy!"

Chapter III

Jim walked around the block before meeting Archie for checkers. He tried missing every crack in the old sidewalk, pretending he was nine again. Oh, what a fun time it was, he reminisced. Simple things meant a great deal. He wondered if Jimmy was just as carefree. He desperately wanted to give the boy a good childhood. Just like his own cherished memories.

Archie looked at his watch, tapping at the crystal with his index finger as Jim strolled up to the table, as if to stress his tardiness.

"I'm only a few minutes late," said Jim.

Jim sat down and made his first move. Fifteen minutes later, a rain drop fell onto one of Archie's pieces.

"Great, just when I was getting ready for the kill."

"Thank God," said Jim.

Archie reached into his canvas tote where he kept his standard issue items for the park: an umbrella, a few cans of Tab, his eyeglass case, a seat cushion and a box of Cracker Jack. But today he brought an extra item. He pulled out a small looking case, which popped open when he pushed a button, revealing a camera lens.

"What the heck is that?" asked Jim.

"I've been looking for an opportunity to try this out. It's a Polaroid SX-70 land camera."

"A whaaaat?"

"Just watch," said Archie.

Archie stood up and leaned over the checker board as he pushed the button. A second later, a small, square paper card shot out from the front of the camera. Archie pulled the card free from the camera.

"Now we just wait," said Archie, as he waved the card back and forth as if he was fanning himself.

"Helps to circulate the chemicals as it's processing. Says so in the instructions," he stated, as Jim sat there with a disgusted face. Archie then tucked the photo under his arm pit.

"Needs to also be warmed," said Archie.

"Are you gonna burp it and put it to bed next?" asked Jim.

"Ha, very funny. Now watch..."

Archie held the photo in front of Jim. Jim looked over his glasses and watched as the colors grew a bit more vivid. All he said was "Huh."

"There. Now we can pack up before it starts to pour and pick up where we left off tomorrow," said Archie.

"That thing stinks," said Jim. "It's not bad enough you kick my butt in this game just about every day, but now you're going to preserve the moment with a stinky picture, just so you can gloat?"

"I'm not gloating," Archie shot back. "Just making it so we can start at the same spot tomorrow."

Jim laughed with Archie and then happened to glance at his Timex.

"Oh crap, the school bus. I'm supposed to meet Jimmy. He's got a half-day."

No sooner had the words come out of his mouth, when he heard the squeal of the bus's brakes from across the park.

The rain started to pick up a little and Jim stood up.

"See ya tomorrow Arch, gotta go."

"Hang on," said Archie, as he dumped the checkers game into his tote and opened his umbrella. It was red vinyl with the word Schlitz screen-printed across it about a hundred times.

"What the heck is that?" said Jim. "I didn't know you drank Schlitz."

"I do now. I switched from Bud a few weeks back. Some guy brought a box of stuff into the shop the other day and I thought the umbrella was pretty cool. Come on, there's room under here for both of us."

"Are you kidding? We'll look like a couple of patsies waltzing across the green under that thing. I got my cap; I'm fine."

Jim pulled down his wool tweed cap so it covered his glasses as much as possible. He hated it when his glasses got wet.

As the two men walked across the green and the bus pulled away with the usual lingering gray diesel cloud, Jim could see young Jimmy having some sort of trouble with another kid. A much bigger kid than little Jimmy. The big kid had Jimmy by the front of his jacket and was pulling him up close, so Jimmy was almost on his tip toes and looking quite scared.

"Wait here pal," said Jim. "I'll be right back."

Archie did as he was told and relit his pipe under the protection of his Schlitz umbrella.

Jim didn't know the kid's name, but he's seen him around the block. He was a neighborhood "tough-guy" who hung out with his other leather jacket-clad friends, smoking on the street corner to look cool, but also because he probably wasn't tough enough to do it in front of his old man.

Jim couldn't hear what they were saying, but as he got closer he could tell by the tone it was of a threatening nature.

"When I ask you for your lunch tomorrow, you better open that box. You got it?"

Jimmy looked terrified and dropped his Kung Fu lunch box. It popped open as it hit the ground and his thermos rolled out onto the grass.

Just then there was a loud slap. The kind of slap when a large hand comes down on a leather jacket.

The kid turned around and then looked up to see big Jim Dillon standing over him.

Jim grabbed the kid's jacket lapels and pulled him up close. He always enjoyed giving bullies a taste of their own medicine.

"Listen up punk! You stay the hell away from my grandson or by God I'll plunsh..." Plunsh??

Jim had felt his upper false teeth give way and were slowly sliding out of his mouth until he only held them in check with his lips.

The bully's eyes opened wide and he pulled his head back as far away from Jim as he could, as if he was avoiding some disease.

Jim let go of the kid and spit the teeth into one of his hands. A long string of spit hung off his lower lip. "GROSS!!!" yelled the bully, who turned and ran away across the green toward the north side of town.

"Sum-o-da-bith," whispered Jim through his gums.

He wiped off the teeth and popped them back into place as best he could. He then picked up the thermos and put it back in the Kung Fu lunch box, then handed it to Jimmy.

"Come on pal," said Jim. "Let's head home. I'll make us both a nice peanut butter and jelly sandwich with a big glass of milk."

As they walked back across the green in the rain, Archie turned and walked with them.

"Put the fear of God into him I see."

"Shut up, Arch," said Jim, laughing to himself.

When grandfather and grandson reached the front steps of their apartment, Jimmy gave his grandpa a hug.

"Thanks, Grandpa," said Jimmy, and then wiped his feet on the mat before walking inside and hanging up his coat and cap on the coat rack in the hall.

"Anytime," said Jim, who smiled back.

Walking into the kitchen, Jim pulled the peanut butter and jelly down from the cabinet. As the two ate their sandwiches, Jim thought to ask more about the other boy, but decided it best to just let Jimmy bring up the topic when he felt the time was right. Instead, he asked about Mrs. Allen to see if Jimmy had anything to report on her ill-tempered ways. Jimmy filled him in on the details.

After their snack, Jimmy pulled out his homework and started to write at the kitchen table. Every so often he stopped to erase a word or two and rewrite them. Jim sat back and watched him without saying anything. It was interesting in a relaxing sort of way. Kind of like when he sat in the barber chair over at Luigi's and watched him work in the mirror on his gray mop. Something was just mesmerizing about the whole experience of watching Jimmy's mind work as he wrestled with certain words, and then once again erase and correct.

Jimmy broke the silence as he looked up at Jim. "Grandpa, do you think there is music in heaven?"

The question came out of left field, but Jim handled it smoothly.

"Sure, I believe so. Angels have those harps, don't they? Why do you ask?"

"Well, our homework for writing this week was to come up with a question we weren't sure of, and then write about what we thought the answer might be. I was thinking about Dad, and how he loved to play his records on the stereo."

"Wow, you remember that?"

"Sure. I remember how he sometimes would sing, too."

"Yes, he did. Your dad loved his records. Sometimes he'd pick you up in his arms and dance around the room with you. You'd break into a deep belly laugh that had us all cracking up."

"I miss him a lot," said Jimmy.

"I do too," said Jim. But I know he's really proud of you and sees all the great things you do."

"You think so, Grandpa?"

"I know so," said Jim.

"What kind of music did you dance to, Grandpa?"

"Well, to be honest, I never was really much of a dancer."

"But Archie said last week that when you boxed, you used to dance around the ring. I hope it wasn't disco, because that's for girls."

"No, it wasn't disco," Jim laughed. "Dancing in boxing means shuffling your feet, so you keep your balance at all times."

"Oh, I didn't know that," said Jimmy, as he flipped his pencil over again and started erasing.

"Yeah, I'm sure your dad has his music in heaven, pal."

"Do you think you could teach me how to box?" asked Jimmy.

Jim once again 'donned his glove' to make the catch from left field.

"Well, uh, I think schooling and homework is more important than learning how to box, but I thought it was Kung Fu you wanted to learn?"

"I thought about it and I'd rather learn from you. I bet no one picked on you when you went to school."

"Well, we had bullies too, when I went to school."

"You did? What did you do?"

"Mostly steered clear of them. Sometimes my friends and I would take a route home from school where we could avoid them. But there was always a group of us that walked home together, so I guess you could say we had strength in numbers. But it's important to remember that no one is born a bully. Something happens to make them that way. I figure they got picked on themselves at one point in their lives and they just pass their anger onto others by bullying someone else."

"You mean that kid on the school bus probably got picked on?

"Most likely, or maybe his family situation isn't quite right. But think of it this way... You know that show we watch that you like so much, called Kung Fu?"

"Yeah, it's one of my favorites. He's a great fighter."

"Well, that guy who plays the main character isn't just a great fighter, he's usually teaching others how a good act can have a positive effect on others. And he's right, it usually does. So that way you don't carry that anger inside and become a bully yourself."

"Did you ever get in a fight when you were a kid?"

"Sure, a few times. But only when it was unavoidable."

"I bet I could shuffle my feet pretty fast," said Jimmy.

"I'm sure you could, but homework first, pal."

Jim paused for a moment, then added, "Maybe I can show you a few moves on the weekend if your homework is all done."

"Thanks!" said Jimmy, who went back to finishing his paper.

Jim smiled, laughing to himself as he remembered Jimmy's words and pictured his younger self, literally dancing around the boxing ring to music, in his signature satin green shorts.

Chapter IV

The large chestnut tree on the green cast its shadow upon Jim and Archie, who were sitting in their usual morning spot. Jim sat with a nonchalant, cross-legged posture in front of the checker board with the morning paper held open, pretending not to notice the predicament his pieces were in.

Suddenly Jim shouted, "I've got it!"

"You've got what?" asked Archie. "My kings have you cornered. Put the paper down and just make your move already!"

"I know how to help with Jimmy's free time this summer. I'm going to get him a paper route. Look here; it says route for sale. Fifty-five customers in the south downtown area from Main down to Chestnut Street. Hey, that covers your block. You'll be one of Jimmy's customers, Arch. I'm gonna call the number."

"How 'bout you make your move first, so we can finish the game; then call the number."

Jim gave the board a glance but then looked back at Archie and kept talking. "It's gonna be great, Arch. I had a route as a kid, and not only did it keep me busy, it was great comic book and baseball card money. I think I even paid for my first bike with my Christmas tips."

"Sounds good, Jim. Here's a tip: Make your move!"

"Okay, fine!"

Jim jumped one of Archie's black pieces and took his paltry reward. Before Jim could even place the piece down on the table, Archie triple jumped his remaining pieces with one of his three kings.

"There. Now you can make your call."

Jim just shook his head in disgust. "Come on, I'll put some coffee on. I picked up a box of Benny's freshly made doughnuts this morning."

The two packed up their board and walked back toward Jim's apartment.

"I think I want to be the black pieces next time we play."

"No way. I'm always black. You're red," said Archie.

Jim just looked at Archie again and shook his head.
"I didn't think you were superstitious."

"I'm not superstitious, I just like tradition."

When the school bus dropped off Jimmy that afternoon, Jim was waiting with a big smile on his face and one of Benny's fresh doughnuts in a bag.

"Here ya' go pal, freshly made this morning."

Jimmy opened the bag and grinned.

"My favorite, chocolate frosted! Thanks Grandpa," said Jimmy.

"You know how we were talking about your summer break, which is coming up soon?" asked Jim.

"Yes. Are we going on vacation?"

"Well, not exactly. I mean, we can certainly plan a few day trips. Maybe to the amusement park or the beach. But I wanted to talk with you about your free time."

"My free time?"

"Yeah, you know. Like when you're watching cartoons or reading a comic. Free time. You're going to have a lot of it this summer and, well, I thought a guy your age might like a part-time job of sorts. You know, for some extra mad money."

"You mean like when Walter Fisher mows his dad's lawn every Saturday? He told me he gets fifty cents allowance."

"Yeah, kind of like that. Only we don't have a lawn. I was thinking more like... a paper route."

"You mean I'd have to deliver papers on my own?"

"Well, yes. But we'd do it together for a while, just until you learned all of the customers on the route. I found one close to home and it's only weekdays, so your weekends will be free. I had a route as a kid, and I guarantee you'll make much more than Walter Fisher."

"How much more?"

"Well, the ad in the paper says fifty-five customers, so you'd probably make about fifteen-or-so dollars a week, plus tips!"

"I'll be rich!" shouted Jimmy.

"Yes," Jim laughed. "But more importantly, you'll get experience and be learning an important responsibility. Your customers will be counting on you to be on time, and Archie is even one of your customers."

"Well, how will I get the route? I mean, what does it cost?"

"I already spoke to the owner on the phone who is selling the route. He's had the route for several years and is heading off to college. I'll purchase the route and you can pay me back after you earn back the money. How's that sound?"

"Sounds like a plan, Gramps," Jimmy said with his mouth full of doughnut.

The following Tuesday, Jimmy started his afternoon paper route. Jim had picked up two bundles of papers from the street corner where a van had deposited them on the sidewalk.

He took out his pocket knife, split the plastic cord and helped Jimmy transfer one of the bundles of papers to his canvas bag.

"Wow, these are heavy, Grandpa," he said as he pulled the bag strap over his shoulder.

"You'll get so strong over time, you won't even notice," Jim replied.

"We'll leave the other bundle here and come back for it later. That way you can split up the route by the different streets and you won't have to carry all the papers at one time."

They walked from house to house, leaving a newspaper on each doorstep. Jim showed Jimmy the map he had drawn of the neighborhood blocks, which detailed the mix of two and three story houses, and the couple of apartment buildings where there would be multiple customers.

When they reached the end of the block, Jim checked the customer list and saw it was the first of a few three-story houses.

He read aloud: "Mrs. Giovanni, 128 Maple Avenue, third floor."

"I'm gonna show you a neat trick,"said Jim. "I used to be able to toss these pretty darn accurate."

"Won't it open up and fly all over the place?" asked Jimmy.

"Naaa, the trick is all in how you fold it. Now watch closely."

Jim folded the paper in thirds and tucked the leading edge under the first fold. With an outward toss and a flip of the wrist, he threw it upward toward the third-story porch. What initially looked like a good toss continued to sail past the porch and up onto the roof.

"Is there someone living up on the roof, Grandpa?" asked Jimmy.

"Uh, no. Here, give me another one."

Jim proceeded to make another fold and tossed it slightly lower this time.

It landed on the porch, but not before ricocheting off Mrs. Giovanni's tomato plant and knocking one of her not-yet-ripe Better Boys off the vine. It fell from the third floor porch, and down onto the sidewalk with a splat.

Mrs, Giovanni grew her tomatoes in a green house during the early spring and by early summer, she would put her red beauties out on the porch during sunny warm days.

"Oh, man... Maybe we'll try throwing another time," said Jim.

Just then, Mrs Giovanni came out on the porch and stood over the railing.

"What-a you do?" she shouted, as she leaned over the porch railing and stared down at Jim, who felt like he was being a scolded by his mom.

"Uh, the boy... I mean, uh, I was teaching my grandson how to toss papers."

"Maybe you should teach him to walk up-a the stairs' eh?" she retorted.

"I'll be sure to get you another tomato from the market Mrs. Giovanni, I promise."

"That's okay, just-a make-a sure the boy uses the stairs from-a now on."

"Oh, I will. You can count on that."

Jim, who was now red in the face, turned to walk away expecting Jimmy to follow.

Jimmy tugged at his grandfathers sleeve.

" Grandpa, what about the paper on the roof?"

"That will be Archie's paper and we'll just share ours with him if he asks. I'm sure he won't mind."

All that week, Jimmy walked with his grandfather and was getting good at remembering each and every stop he needed to make.

It was Thursday of the following week when Jimmy needed to collect from his customers. He had decided he wanted to do it alone. Some of the customers had told Jimmy in advance where they would leave the money, like under the door mat or in their mailbox. Some waited until Jimmy came and rang the bell or knocked, so they could give Jimmy some feedback on his timeliness - or lack thereof. It was on the third floor of an apartment building on Maple Avenue when Jimmy got a surprise after he knocked on the door. It took a few seconds for someone to answer, and he could hear footsteps running toward the door, and then it opened. The chain was still attached on the inside of the door, allowing it to open only a few inches. A petite face peered out through the crack.

"Dad... paperboy!" the voice yelled.

Jimmy could hear the response from further inside.

"Money's on the counter. Pay him, please."

The door closed again for a second and Jimmy could hear the footsteps run away, and then back again. This time he heard the unchaining of the lock. The door opened and there stood a little blonde-haired girl with green eyes. Her hair was in a pony tail and she was wearing denim overalls. The kind he had seen painters often wear.

"Hi! Here ya go," she said, holding out the crinkled dollar in her fist.

Jimmy stood in a daze for a moment. He wasn't sure what had come over him. He didn't really like girls, but he felt different this time.
He opened his hand and she dropped the crinkled dollar into it.

"Hold on," she said, as she ran back inside.

Jimmy wasn't going anywhere. He just stood and waited as he was asked. The girl ran back and handed Jimmy a cookie.

"Here. My mom just baked these."

It was chocolate chip. Jimmy's favorite.

"Thanks," said Jimmy. "I'm Jimmy Dillon."

"I'm Sam. Sam Olsen. My real name is Samantha, but my family and friends call me Sam."

"Hi Sam," said Jimmy. "You go to Franklin Elementary school?" It was the only thing that came into his head.

"Yes, I'm in fourth grade. How about you?"

"I'm in fourth, too. Mrs. Allen's class."

"I hear she's kinda strict," said Sam.

"You have no idea. No talking in class. Can't watch the clock or doodle. That kinda stuff."

"Well, I gotta set the table for dinner. See you next week," said Sam.
"Yeah, sure. See you next week. Oh, and thanks for the cookie."

Jimmy had finished the cookie before he reached the sidewalk.

He wondered how he had never seen Sam in the hallway at school.

But when he really thought about it, he had never paid much attention to any of the girls in his school. He always felt they weren't really worth talking to.

None of them ever wanted to play army or tag during recess, and he hadn't seen any of them in the comic book store.

But Sam seemed different. 'Kinda nice,' he thought.

At home, Jimmy counted his collections at the kitchen table and subtracted his earnings from the money to pay the newspaper.

"Fourteen dollars, Grandpa!"

"Hey, that's fantastic," shouted Jim as he stirred the spaghetti over the stove.

"I still have a few houses to collect from, but I should be able to get the remainder later this week."

"Sounds like a plan, Jimmy. I told you math would come in handy some day."

"Met a new friend today, Gramps. Got a cookie, too."

"What's his name?" asked Jim.

"Sam," answer Jimmy. "But it isn't a him, it's uh, a girl."

"A girl?" Jim answered, surprised.

"Well yeah. I mean, she wasn't gross or anything. Not like that fat Martha Butler who ate my lunch that time. Sam is much cooler."

"Well, cool is good," replied Jim. "Maybe you can ask her over some time."

"Over here?" asked Jimmy.

"Yeah, here, as in where we live. Anything wrong with that?"

"Well no, Grandpa, just that, well, what if... I don't know."

Jim Duggan knew his grandson well. So well, in fact, that at times it was as if their thoughts were in complete alignment.

Jimmy had friends he played with over the years, but it was always outside or at school. He had never brought anyone back to the apartment to watch cartoons or share his comics.

"So you think she might think it's funny that you live with your grandpa? Is that it, pal?"

Jimmy looked out the window as if he was searching for an answer when he already knew his grandpa was close to the truth.

"Sort of. But not because I live with you. More like, because... I don't have a mom or dad. I mean, what do I do when she asks me why my mom and dad aren't home?"

"Just like always, Jimmy, you give her an honest answer."

Jim turned off the spaghetti on the stove and sat down next to his grandson.

"There are lots of kids that have different families, Jimmy. There are some kids that have both parents at home, but not a loving household. The most important thing to remember is not who raises you, but that you are loved. And I'm so proud of you. I know your dad is proud of you, too. He smiles down from heaven on you, lad."

"I know he does, Grandpa. But my mom..."

"Your mom was a confused young lady, Jimmy. Believe me, if she came back today, I'd welcome her back into our family with open arms. But I have no idea where she is, and it's been such a long time. We have each other though, and I'll be here for you. I'm not going anywhere soon. I promise. When you decide the time is right, you can introduce me to your new friend, Sam, and maybe we can even have her over for spaghetti some evening."

Jimmy hopped off his chair and hugged his grandpa around his waist as far as his arms could reach. Jim took out his hanky and lifted Jimmy's chin so he could dry his eyes.

"You've got your summer vacation starting next week. Whaddaya say we head down to the comic store on Saturday and get you half a dozen comics? I might buy one myself. It's been a while since I put my feet up and read a good western. We can even stop at Benny's for some fresh doughnuts."

"It's a deal, Grandpa," said Jimmy, smiling.

Chapter V

Archie had a mouthful of Oreo cookies when Jim and Jimmy walked into his "Lost and Found Treasures" antique store.

"Got any new baseball cards, Arch? I mean, new old ones, that is."

Archie paused while he took a gulp from his can of Schlitz.

"A few. Some guy dumped his collection here last week, but they were mostly doubles of what I had. He also turned in a catcher's mitt, in case Jimmy is interested."

Archie put the shoebox of cards and the catcher's mitt on the counter and took another sip of Schlitz.

"Normal people drink milk with these, Arch," said Jim, as he tossed one of Archie's Oreos into his mouth."

"Here, take a look through these, Jimmy," said Archie. "See if you can find any you'd like."

Jim placed the mitt on his hand and pounded his large fist into the leather a few times. It made a nice sharp pop each time.

"Nothin' like a well-worn glove. I'd take one of these over a new one any day. Already oiled and broken in. Doesn't look like the previous owner chewed the laces much either."

"That's 'cus he was busy, as catchers are. It's the fielders who chew their laces, Jim," said Archie. "Ain't that right, Jimmy?"

Jimmy looked up from the shoebox full of cards.

"Yeah. Last spring we had a kid chew his glove so bad, he tried to snag a deep fly ball and it fell apart in the middle. The ball went right through it and gave him a fat lip. Coach McFadden took the glove home and re-laced it for him."

"I'd rather chew Oreos," said Archie. "Want one, Jimmy?"

"No thanks, Mr. Reynolds. I just had a couple of doughnuts. Hey! Here's a Carlton Fisk. Can I get this one, Gramps?"

"It's your paper route money, Jimmy. You can spend it on whatever you like."

"Oh, yeah, I forgot. I'm just used to asking, that's all."

Jimmy reached into his pocket and pulled out a small handful of change. "How much for the Carlton Fisk, Mr. Reynolds?"

"I'll tell ya what; you can pick out four more and hand me a dime... or you can take the whole box home for fifty cents. How's that sound?"

"Sounds like a deal!"

Jimmy handed Archie the fifty cents and put the lid on his new box of trophies and placed it on the counter.

"You mind if I poke around some more, Grandpa?"

"No, you go right ahead, lad."

Jimmy walked down one of the aisles, looking inside boxes and trying on old hats. He had loved coming into Archie's antique shop ever since he was four years old. Gramps and his dad, Danny, would come in to shoot the breeze with Archie, and Jimmy would lose himself in the aisles of treasure, which harkened back to a mysterious older time.

It was a good size store and Archie kept the inventory flowing. He was always fair with his prices, so there were always plenty of new items for Jimmy to poke through.

"That was very generous, Archie," said Jim. "That box should have brought you a few bucks at the very least."

"Right back at ya, pal. I just love seeing the smile on Jimmy's face. I still have my card and comic collections. It's something about the journey, ya know. It's all about looking for the ones you're missing. Then there's the smell when you open the box. It hits you like you just entered the store for the first time."

Jim reached into his back pocket and pulled out a folded comic. "We actually stopped at the comic store today. Picked myself up Gunsmoke, featuring Kid Colt! Going to read it tonight before I hit the hay."

Both Archie and Jim laughed out loud at their juvenile attitudes.

"Hey, Jim. I was thinking about you mentioning looking for things for Jimmy to do, to keep himself busy. I know he's got the afternoon paper route, but since he's on his summer break, maybe... that is, if you would allow it... maybe he could come in and help me organize during the morning hours. I'd pay him for his time and he just loves this place, ya know."

"That's not a bad idea. For him it would be like work, but not really. You go ahead and ask him, Archie. It's okay with me, pal. Just make sure he doesn't see you drinking a bunch of that beer. He's at an impressionable age, ya know."

Jim took another Oreo and popped it in his mouth and smiled at Archie. Archie took his Schlitz can and put it under the counter out of sight. When Jimmy walked back to the counter, Archie asked him about helping out in the shop a few days a week, sorting and displaying items.

Jimmy looked up at his grandpa and motioned with his finger for Jim to lean closer. As he did, Jimmy whispered something in his ear.

"Well, I don't know Jimmy, you'll need to ask Archie that question."

"Uh, Mr Reynolds, would it be okay if I brought my friend, Sam, too? She's a girl who lives on my paper route. But she's not mushy like other girls. She tells me she gets tired of helping her mom do chores around the house and I bet she'd like to help in the store."

"Okay," said Archie, "I think I can afford two part-time helpers. Why don't you start Monday morning. I open at ten."

"Thanks, Mr Reynolds, I'll be here. And thanks again for the baseball cards."

"Right back at ya'," replied Archie.

Chapter VI

Monday morning started off bright and sunny, and Sam decided to ride her bike to the apartment where Jimmy and his grandpa lived. She locked her bike on the rack in front, walked inside and rang the buzzer for Jimmy's apartment.

"Hello, this is Jim."

Sam paused for a second, seeming confused. The voice seemed much deeper and older than her new friend's.

"Um, this is Sam, Jimmy."

"Oh, Sam, yes. I'm Jimmy's grandpa. He told me you were stopping by. I'll buzz you in."

Sam walked down the hallway where Jimmy was waiting by the door. Sam handed a small paper bag to Jimmy.

"Chocolate chip, my favorite! Thanks, Sam. Would you like to come in and meet my grandpa? He used to be a boxer when he was younger, but now he's just a grandpa. He's a really nice guy."

"Sure," said Sam.

Jim smiled as the two young kids walked in. As cute as he thought them to be, he remembered to play it cool and not embarrass his grandson.

"Hello Sam, I'm Jim Dillon, Jimmy's grandpa."

Sam reached out to shake Jim's hand and was amazed at the size of his huge paw. It was clearly larger than her mom or dad's hand. She smiled after realizing her hand was not going to be crushed.

"So I hear you two are going to help Archie, I mean Mr. Reynolds, sort out some of his junk... uh, I mean antiques."

"Yes," said Sam. " Jimmy told me there's all kinds of interesting old things in his store."

"We should be home by noon, Gramps. Plenty of time before my papers arrive," said Jimmy.

The two walked out the door and down the steps to where Sam's bike was.

"Wow, that's a nice bike," said Jimmy.

"Thanks. My parents got it for my birthday. I like the handbrakes and tassels on the handlebars best of all. Do you have a bike?"

"No, I had one when I was younger, but I outgrew it. Gramps and I pretty much walk everywhere together. But don't worry. If you ride, I can jog alongside of you. "

"I have a better idea, we can both sit on the banana seat if I pedal and you hop on back."

"Sure, I guess I can try that."

Jimmy felt a little funny at first sitting on the back of his friend's bike as she peddled, especially if any of the other guys saw him on a bike with tassels on the handlebars. But this was different. He really liked Sam and as he held onto her shoulders, she pushed off and got her balance.

Sam rode extra slow so as not to lose Jimmy off the back of the bike. At the end of every block, they would stop and each eat a cookie. By the time they reached Lost and Found Treasures, the bag of chocolate chip cookies was reduced to only a few crumbs.

Sam locked her bike up in front of the store. Jimmy remembered what his grandpa said about being a gentleman, and held the door for Sam as they both walked inside.

"Hi, Mr. Reynolds," said Jimmy. "This is my friend, Sam. She's going to help me work on sorting out your stuff."

"Hi, Sam," replied Archie. "Glad you can help. I figure I can pay you each fifty cents an hour while you're here, and if you find something you like while your working, we can work out a deal for that, too."

Archie then gave Jimmy and Sam a list of items to find in the back room, which was long overdue to be sorted. Some of the items would need to be cleaned off, too, having been stored in some people's attics or garages. Archie would then price and display the items on the shelves in the front portion of the store.

"Now if you have any questions on what an item is, just come up front and ask... and please be careful back there. That stuff is piled up pretty high. There's a table with some empty boxes you can use to sort similar items."

"We'll be careful, Mr Reynolds," said Jimmy.

When Jimmy and Sam walked past the shop aisles and into the back room, they could see exactly what Archie meant when he said overflowing. There were piles of records, sporting equipment, glass vases and tea sets, metal toy trains and trucks, clothing racks and boxes stacked upon other boxes, each filled with items Archie had brought in on consignment or back from estate sales he attended.

In the only corner of the room that wasn't overcrowded with stuff, was a table with a stack of empty boxes. Jimmy took one of the boxes and asked Sam what was first on the list.

"Let's see," said Sam, as she looked over the list. "The first item listed is shoes."

Jimmy and Sam started looking through the stacked boxes and found old loafers, ladies high heels, tap dancing shoes and some cowboy boots with holes worn right through the soles. Thirty minutes passed by before Jimmy and Sam began to laugh at some of the shoes. Jimmy noticed that he could fit his sneakers right inside some of the large loafers. He then took a large bow tie from one of the boxes and held it up to his neck.

"Look Sam, I'm a circus clown." Jimmy walked around, making a big slapping sound when the size twelve shoes hit the floor with each step.

Sam giggled out loud. "Who knew we'd have fun sorting old, stinky shoes?"

Jimmy pinched his nose as he made a squished face and dropped the loafers into the box. Sam agreed it would be best to move down the list.

"Ooo.. Next item is jewelry," said Sam, as her eyes lit up a bit.

Jimmy didn't find that any more exciting than the old shoes, but he could see that it interested Sam, so they started in. The two worked well together, and by noon they had worked their way partially down the list as they boxed up the jewelry, shoes, metal toys and old books.

"What's next on the list?" asked Sam.

"Records," replied Jimmy. "It says: Please sort by last name or name of band. This looks like it could take some time. I think we should head home for lunch. I have to start my paper route in the afternoon. Would you like to eat over at our place? My grandpa makes a super peanut butter and jelly sandwich."

"Sure," said Sam.

Jimmy and Sam carried a few boxes up to the front counter and Archie paid Jimmy and Sam each a dollar for their work.

"You two did alright. I hope to see you tomorrow."

"Sure thing," said Jimmy.

The two walked back to Jimmy's apartment and Jim made them each a peanut butter and jelly sandwich accompanied by a big glass of milk. He then went into the den to give them some privacy.

Sam took a big gulp of milk and wiped the mustache from her upper lip. "If we work through Friday, we'll each have five dollars," said Sam. "What are you going to do with your share?"

"Well, I've been thinking that maybe I should save up my money for a new bike; that way we can ride together. How about you?"

"I like music, so maybe some new records. My mom and dad got me and my brother a new record player last Christmas. We both share it.

Who knows, maybe I'll find some good ones when we sort through the box at Mr Reynolds' tomorrow."

"My dad loved records. Mostly rock and roll, but some older ones, too, from when he was young. Sometimes he'd sing when he was cooking dinner for me and Gramps."

Jimmy then got quiet for a minute and took a large gulp of milk.

"You okay?" asked Sam.

"Yeah, I'm okay. Just that sometimes I really miss him. Not that my grandpa isn't great; it's just that he's 'gramps' and my dad was, well... different. He was my dad. But he died of cancer, and since then it's just been me and Gramps."

"What about your mom?" asked Sam.

"She left my dad and me when I was very little. I don't really remember her at all. Gramps said she was just confused with what she was looking for in life, 'cus she was very young. We don't know where she is. Gramps said he tried looking for her once and even hired somebody to help us look, but she wasn't in the city. She must have gone far away."

"Sorry," said Sam. "It must be hard not having a mom."

"That's okay. Like I said, it's just me and Gramps now, and we make out fine."

"Well, you were right. He certainly makes dynamite peanut butter and jelly sandwiches," said Sam.

Jimmy smiled at Sam as he polished off his milk.

The two got along really well over the next several days. Sam even offered to use her bike to help Jimmy deliver papers on his route.

Jimmy would give her a bunch of papers, which she would place on her bike rack, and head down one side of the street. Jimmy would use his paper bag and run down the other side.

Jimmy would often look across the street to see if he was ahead of Sam or falling behind. He always remembered to run up Mrs. Giovanni's stairs and not toss the paper all the way to the top.

When they got done with the route, they would sometimes go down to the bakery and get a couple of doughnuts. Sometimes they would go to the green and lay on their backs under the large oak or maple trees and talk about their favorite cartoons and movies.

Jimmy had taught Sam how to climb trees, and sometimes they would climb their favorite maple tree, which had branches spiraling up the trunk and was at least fifty feet tall. They would each find a branch that looked comfortable and sit up high while leaning back, watching the clouds above and feeling the wind sway the tree back and forth. They would both hang on tight and laugh when a good gust came by.

Having a friend like Sam to pal around with turned out to be the best thing to happen to Jimmy in a long time. He was glad she lived so close by, and that she didn't have to be dropped off like some of his other friends. The more time they spent together, the more they found they had in common.

He wasn't sure if this is what it felt like to have a sister, or maybe even a girlfriend. All he knew was that he wanted the summer to last forever, so he could see Sam every day.

Chapter VII

The next week, Jimmy and Sam were back at work in Archie's storage room, when Archie wheeled in a used bike.

"I really appreciate how hard you kids are working. It's easier minding the store without having to constantly run up to the front counter every time someone comes in."

Archie put the kickstand down on the bike and squatted beside it as he lifted the back wheel off the ground with one hand and rotated the pedals with the other. He listened to the clicking of the chain as the back wheel spun.

"Hmm. Needs the gear cable adjusted and the back tire is flat, and I think these brake pads need replacing too. But I should be able to get it running well by next week."

Jimmy placed the records he was sorting back into the box. The Big Bopper and Elvis would just have to wait. The dirt and dust could not conceal the beauty of the deep, emerald green cycle to Jimmy's youthful eyes. It was a Schwinn Stingray, with a silver sparkle, high-back banana seat, hand brakes, and the highly coveted three-speed shifter, which shot forth from a box on the top of the frame like the stick on a fighter jet. It was just like the one he saw in the ad in the back pages of his comic books.

"Is that for sale, Mr Reynolds?" Jimmy asked.

His voice was soft, almost timid, as he feared the bike might be spoken for.

"Well, yes. I actually just bought it for a pretty good price, given that it's seven years old and needs some work."

"How much are you going to sell it for?"

"Well, I was going to ask around thirty-two dollars for it. These go for about fifty dollars new. Of course, if a shrewd young man wanted to haggle, the price could come down some."

Jimmy knew what the word meant, but he had never haggled over anything before, except maybe staying up late on the weekend so he could have more 'comic book time' before turning out his light. He also remembered his grandpa returning a box of cookies to the grocery store once when they discovered most of the box was broken, but that was different.

Archie stared at Jimmy as he bit his bottom lip, looking like he was about to say something, but no words came out. He just kept staring at the green Stingray.

Unbeknownst to Jimmy, Jim had already spoke to Archie about Jimmy wanting to get a bike, and he had asked Archie to keep his eye out for a good bike, should one come into the store.

"I tell you what," said Archie. "If you know of someone interested... I mean really interested, I suppose I could take twenty-five dollars for it."

Jimmy's face beamed.

"I'm gonna ask Gramps, Mr. Reynolds. Would you hold it for me?"

"I already was figuring to do just that, Jimmy. Tell Big Jim it will help you on your paper route."

Archie patted Jimmy on the shoulder and walked back to the front of the store.

"Wow," said Sam. "That's a really dynamite bike."

"It sure is. Once Archie and I get it fixed up, you and I will be able to ride places together."

"Sounds like a plan," said Sam.

Sam dug into the box of records, to start looking for any she might like, but Jimmy had already been mystically transported to a high-speed race on an asphalt track.

Legs peddling as fast as he could muster. The bright orange pole flag attached to his banana seat, waving in the wind. The Butch Hobson baseball card, attached to the rear fender with a wooden clothespin, flapped wildly with a roar, as the gleaming spokes spun round and round.

Competition was gaining on him, but no Huffy or Columbia could match the speed of the mighty Stingray. With a thrust of his hand, Jimmy threw the patented Stik-shift forward into third gear, launching himself far past the competition and across the finish line. As the dust cleared, he slowed himself by down shifting and applying his silky-smooth hand brakes.

Of course, a victory lap was in order, and he waved to the crowd. Gramps and Sam were in the front row of the grandstand, cheering as he rode past. Archie sipped on his Schlitz, waving.

"Come on, Jimmy! Come on!..."

"Hello... Jimmy, are you going to help me sort these?"

Jimmy was suddenly transported back into Archie's storage room, looking at Sam who held a bunch of LPs in her hands.

"Yes, of course," said Jimmy. "I was just figuring how much I could put toward the bike from my paper route money."

The rest of the afternoon was spent putting the records in alphabetical order, with Sam correcting Jimmy a few times. Putting M before N was of little importance compared to the words he was preparing for his selling speech to Grandpa.

When they finished sorting, Jimmy noticed that Sam had placed five records off to her side.

"You gonna ask Archie about those?" Jimmy inquired, pointing to the small pile.

"Yup, I was hoping to bring these home."

"Which ones are they?"

"A couple of Partridge Family, an Elvis Presley, a Jackson Five and some lady named Sherri Summer. I don't know her songs, but the front of the album looks really nice."

"Jimmy looked at the front of the album that featured a very pretty picture of a woman with light brunette hair, sitting in a field with lots of flowers surrounding her.

"Looks kinda' girly," Jimmy said.

"Uh, yah. I'm a girl," said Sam. "Besides, I bet it's really nice. I'm going to play it as soon as I get home."

Sam and Jimmy settled up with Archie, each putting their hard-earned pay in their pockets, and Sam eagerly tucking her albums on her back bicycle rack in anticipation of listening to them.

When Sam arrived home, she couldn't wait to play her records. Looking into her brother's room, she could see him playing army with his G.I. Joe action figures.

"The perfect time to have the record player to myself," she thought.

She picked up the unit by the handle from their family room and set it up in her bedroom, closing the door for extra privacy. Listening to a new album wasn't just a short-lived experience. It was normally a journey that started by reading the liner notes with a glass of milk and some cookies and then progressed to dropping the needle on the record as she followed along with the lyrics, which were usually printed on the album cover sleeve. This time was proving to be slightly different, for when Sam pulled the the Jackson Five album from the sleeve and placed it on the turntable, she noticed the arm of the player was missing the needle.

She looked around the unit, thinking it might have fallen out and gotten lodged under the edge of the spinning turntable, but it was nowhere to be found. She opened her door and ran out to the family room, looking to see if it could be on the rug. It was the fear of any child who might have dropped something small on the rug that it would soon fall victim to the vacuum cleaner. Sam scanned the shag carpet with her eyes and even ran her hand across the fuzzy carpet fibers. Still no needle.

Then she ran back to her brother's room and knocked on his door. Eddy was only seven years old, but had a low grumbly voice when it came to playing with his G.I. Joes.

"What," yelled Eddy, thinking it might be his mom asking him to come to dinner.

"It's me, Eddy," said Sam. "Did you play with the record player today?"

Eddy looked sheepishly down at the floor and then looked up at Sam, holding his G.I. Joe up toward her and addressed her in the Sergeant's voice.

"Eddy, is on a mission right now and won't be back until later."

"Funny," said Sam. "Come on, did you use it?"

"Yes," answered Eddy.

"Was it working fine?" asked Sam.

"It was when I had my G.I. Joe guy on it."

"What?!" yelled Sam. "You had your doll on it?"

"It's not a doll!" shouted Eddy. "It's an action figure."

"Well, the needle is missing from it," said Sam.

"That's because it broke when it hit my spinning G.I. Joe."

"Aaaaah," shouted Sam in frustration. "Now I can't play my records!"

Sam explained the situation to her mom, who promised to buy a new needle the next time they were at the shopping mall. Sam was frustrated to even wait an hour, much less to wait until the next time they went to the mall. The Jackson Five and Elvis would just have to wait.

Then Sam's mom made a suggestion she hadn't thought about. "Why don't you bring them over your new friend's house? Maybe he has a record player."

"You think he'd like Elvis?"

"I think a lot of people like Elvis, honey," said her mom, who had a few Elvis records of her own to speak of.

"I'll call him up after dinner and ask," said Sam, who poured herself a glass of milk, grabbed a chocolate chip cookie from the jar and retreated back to her room to enjoy her liner notes and lyrics.

Chapter VIII

Jimmy stared down at the Elvis record as it spun around on the turntable to the sounds of Burning Love.

"You ever try to read the label as it's spinning?" asked Jimmy. "You almost have to blink your eyes and freeze it in your head when it comes around, like you're taking a picture."

"Never tried," said Sam. "I'd probably get dizzy. I prefer to read the lyrics on the sleeve. It's a bummer when they don't come with the lyrics."

"Yeah. I hear ya. There was a song I liked on one of my dad's records and I thought it said, I can see clearly now Lorraine is gone. What it really said was, '..the rain is gone.' For a couple of years I wondered who Lorraine was. I finally read the lyrics and then told Gramps. We had a good laugh. Hey, speaking of Gramps, I'm going to ask if we can have some milk to go with the cookies you brought over. I'll be right back."

As Jimmy got up and walked in the kitchen, Sam changed the record on the turntable to the one that featured the girl on the cover, sitting in a field of flowers. "Okay, Sherri Summer, let's see if you're as good as your picture."

The music started to play and Jimmy came out of the kitchen with two glasses of milk.

"Here ya go, Sam. Now we can dunk them."

Sam took the milk and dunked her cookie, then guzzled a bit down, revealing a milk mustache before she wiped it clean with her shirt sleeve. A true tomboy.

"What happened to Elvis?" asked Jimmy.

"He's great, but I've been so curious about this one. It's actually kind of good."

Jimmy stopped chewing for a moment and listened to the song. It was soft and slow, but not mushy like some of the other girl performers he heard.

"It's pretty good, I guess," he said.

"A Place In My Heart is the name of this one. I like it," Sam said, as she focused on following along with the lyrics on the sleeve.

Jim came out of the kitchen to thank Sam for giving him a couple of cookies to snack on, too, but he decided to wait until the song was over before saying anything. He was so happy that his grandson had a good friend, who seemed to share the same interests as Jimmy. He stood at the edge of the room, just outside the kitchen and listened to the music. There was a softness to her voice, which he liked, but didn't recognize hearing the song before. When the song stopped, he walked over to Jimmy and Sam and asked who they were playing on the stereo.

"It's Sherri Summer," said Sam, who handed the album jacket to Jim.

"Thanks Sam, for the delicious cookies you..." Jim paused as he stared at the front of the jacket, "...for the delicious cookies you brought."

"You're welcome, Mr. Dillon," replied Sam.

"Jim couldn't believe his eyes. He turned the jacket over and walked back into the kitchen. "I'll be right back with this," he said.

Once in the kitchen, he grabbed pencil and pad from the counter and quickly jotted down the name Sherri Summer, then the record company: Sunflower Records, Las Vegas, Nevada.

Walking back to the living room, he handed the record jacket back to Sam, and then did an about-face back to the kitchen. Picking up the telephone, he quickly dialed Archie's number. On the ninth ring, Archie finally picked up.

"I told you I don't want a subscription to Antiques Magazine," shouted Archie.

"Arch, it's Jim," said Jim in a semi-soft whisper.

"Oh, sorry Jim. I thought you were that goofball that already called me twice today. He just won't take no for an answer. Say, you sound hoarse. Are you getting sick?"

"No. I'm whispering so the kids in the living room won't hear me. Now listen, Arch. I need to talk to you. This is important... I think I found Terri."

Chapter IX

The paper route had paid well in tips over the last couple weeks and between that, and working in Archie's store, Jimmy had saved enough for the Stingray bicycle. Gramps let him bring it inside the apartment, where the bike rested on its kickstand just inside the front door. It was a great feeling of freedom to ride the bike around the neighborhood.

Now, Jimmy was about to experience another kind of freedom. A road trip from Philadelphia to Nevada. Gramps said it would take over a week to get there, maybe longer depending on Archie's interference with the itinerary. But since it was the beginning of summer vacation, there would be plenty of time for the trip.

Jimmy's legs pumped as he rounded the corner of the block and headed down to Mrs Giovanni's house. The baseball card, which Jimmy had attached to his fender with a clothespin, made a whirring sound that often gathered a gaze or two from passersby. When he got to her place, he put the kickstand down and ran up the steps, skipping every other one until her reached her door. When he gave a knock, Mrs. Giovanni came to the door with a smile. A wonderful aroma wafted through the open kitchen door and filled Jimmy's nose with delight. Mrs. Giovanni was always baking something wonderful.

"Is it collecting day already?" she asked.

"No, not today, but I brought this for you."

Jimmy reached into his paper bag and pulled out a shiny red tomato. Mrs. Giovanni's face lit up.

"You're a very good boy," she said, taking the tomato from his hand. "Wait-a-here. I will be-a right back."

Mrs. Giovanni came back to the door with a large slice of her spinach pie resting on top of a napkin.

"Here you go. Mangia! "

Jimmy took a bite and thanked Mrs. Giovanni for the wonderful snack. He explained to her, as he did to his other customers, that he'd be going on a vacation for a while, and his friends would cover his route for him.

As he waved goodbye to Mrs. Giovanni, who was still looking down from her porch as he climbed aboard his bike, he thought about Mrs. Giovanni and how her kids must have grown up eating her wonderful cooking. He wondered if his mom was a good cook. He smiled as he thought of how much he loved Gramps... and his signature peanut butter and jelly sandwiches.

When Jimmy got back home, he went to his room and took four Matchbox cars out of the plastic case that held his small collection, and placed them on his dresser. Then he examined each one closely at eye level.

They were four of the more collectible cars he owned, but he thought they would be the icing on the cake to get Mike Savoy to run the first two weeks of his paper route while he was gone. Sam already had agreed she would help when she got back from her summer vacation with her family. Mike lived close by, and Jimmy felt Mike would be a great candidate for the other part of the job. The cars would be extra insurance, just in case the regular weekly pay and Thursday collection tips weren't incentive enough. Mike never could turn down a good Matchbox or Hot Wheels car.

Jim knocked on the door of Jimmy's room, which was answered by a polite, "Come in".

"Hi Jimmy, I thought I'd drop off this duffle bag for you. It was your father's. Should be plenty big enough to hold all the clothes you'll need for the trip. We can stop and do laundry along the way if needed. Oh, and don't forget to pack your toothbrush and comb."

"Thanks, Gramps," said Jimmy. "Is it really over two thousand miles to Las Vegas?"

"Yep. More like twenty-four hundred. I hope the old '57 is up to the task. I changed the oil, along with the plugs and filters, and put new tires on her the other day down at Donnie's garage."

Jimmy smiled. "Sam said she'd cover my route for a couple of weeks when she gets back from vacation with her family. I'm going over to Michael's after dinner, to ask if he'll cover the first part."

Jimmy stuffed the four cars into the front pocket of his jeans.

"Gramps, you think we'll really find my mom?"

Jim had no idea if they'd find her, but kept the conversation positive.

"Well, I look at it this way, we're gonna give it our best shot, and if we don't find her before we have to come back, we'll chalk it up to a fun road trip, pal."

"What if... well, what if we find her and she doesn't want to see me?"

"We have to give her that chance, Jimmy. People change over time and she might not realize how much she really misses you. I have a feeling once she sees you, she's gonna light up like a neon sign. I called the record company on that record label and I guess they got bought by another company a few years back, called Avalon Records."

"Couldn't we call her, Gramps?"

"I thought of that too, pal, but the new recording company said when they called the number they had on file, it was no longer in use. But not to worry. They said they'd ask around to see if she's still in the area. So at least we have some hope."

"I'm gonna' bring that picture of Dad with me too, Gramps. Maybe she misses him, too."

"Maybe so, pal."

Jim walked back to the kitchen and poured himself a glass of milk and took a couple of fig newtons from the cookie jar. He knew it was a long shot that Terri would still be in the area, but it was worth the opportunity to find out. He needed to believe in the words he told Jimmy. He knew his best days were behind him and he worried what would happen to Jimmy, should he pass on before Jimmy was old enough to take care of himself. He just couldn't see Jimmy in a foster home; no way.

He remembered how angry he was when Terri split. He never seemed to have the right words for Danny, to help him get over her leaving. He loved his son with all his heart and swore he'd take care of Jimmy when Danny went into hospice. Now he sees Danny every day in Jimmy's face. But he kept telling himself there's part of Terri in there, too. Jim swallowed the rest of his newton and washed it down with the cold milk.

He asked himself over and over why Terri hadn't come back. What would be the reason to stay away all these years?

Archie had said fear and pride were strong emotions and he guessed that Terri realized it was a mistake, and was probably too afraid to face the family. Maybe Archie was right. Maybe once Terri had the chance to actually meet Jimmy and see what a wonderful kid he was, she'd come back home.

He tried to remain positive for Jimmy's sake. He remembered what his old boxing coach would tell him: "As soon as the bell ends the round, it's in the past. Keep movin', focus on what's in front of you and give it your best shot!"

Chapter X

Archie plopped two large bags beside Jimmy in the back seat of the Bel Air and then climbed in the front passenger seat.

"What is all that? You need two suitcases? I've seen you wear four shirts in the past ten years, and you need two suitcases?"

"Only one is my clothes. I brought my Kodak land camera in case we want to take pictures, some snacks, a six pack of Schiltz and of course the checkers."

"You brought the checkers?"

"Sure. Why not. It's our tradition. I don't want to get rusty."

"I don't know about you sometimes, Arch."

Jim took the bags and put them in the trunk so Jimmy could have more room on the seat, in case he wanted to stretch out during their trip.

"I do need to ask you to please pull up to the pharmacy before we hit the highway. I'm out of toothpaste," said Archie.

"You can use mine, Arch."

I'm not going to use yours. Besides you use that stuff for your dentures. I only use Colgate."

A few minutes later, Jim pulled up in front of Penn's drug store.

"Why don't you go on inside, Arch? Get your Colgate, and while you're at it get one of those ruled pads so we can take notes as we go. My memory isn't what it once was. Get a couple of ballpoint pens, too."

"What color pad should I get?"

"What the heck does that matter, Arch? White, ok? They're all white."

"Actually they're not. They make yellow ones, too, but I'll get white. Do you want anything to drink, Jimmy?"

"Sure, I'll have a Pepsi please, Mr. Reynolds."

"You got it. How about you, Jim?"

"No thanks, Arch. Now please hurry. I'd like to get on the freeway before rush hour hits."

Archie emerged from the drug store with a large paper bag.

"Did you get your toothpaste?" asked Jim.

"Yep, and I got your pad, too, but they only had yellow… and a Pepsi for Jimmy. Plus, a few Charleston Chews and a cool road map."
He handed one of the Charleston Chews to Jimmy, along with the Pepsi and the road map.

"Now you can follow along as we travel across the country, Jimmy. Plus you can bail out Gramps here, when he takes a wrong turn."

"Ha ha, Arch. Very funny. Break me off a piece of that Charleston Chew. I can't bite that stuff with my front dentures."

As Archie wrestled with the candy bar, Jimmy unfolded the road map and looked at all the lines going north to south and east to west. It was like a spider's web.

"Hey, I found Philly," said Jimmy.

"Okay, pal. Plot us a course west," answered Gramps.

For the next few hours, Jimmy was in awe of everything around him. He'd never ridden in Grandpa's old convertible with the top down. Jim wasn't exactly a fast driver and pretty much kept his speed to fifty-five. Jimmy waved from the back seat of the convertible to other cars that passed them on the highway. If it was a truck that passed them, Jimmy would make believe he was pulling the truck horn by pumping his arm up and down; if the driver saw him, they would sometimes respond back with a couple of toots.

Archie popped open a Schlitz just after noon time and the slight spray from the can wafted backwards and felt like a mist on Jimmy's face.

"Want a sip," Archie asked Jimmy as he pretended to pass the can backwards to Jimmy, only to pull it back quickly when Jim barked at him to stop fooling.

"Jeesh," said Archie. "I was only teasing."

Hours later, as the guys entered Ohio on Route 70 west, the sky started to turn gray. Jim looked for a road sign showing where they could grab some dinner and put the top up on the Bel Air.

"Hey, Gramps," shouted Jimmy. "That billboard looks yummy!"

As they drove by, Jim could see large pictures of meat loaf with mashed potatoes and what looked like homemade apple pie. The sign read MEHLMAN'S CAFETERIA.

"Hey, we got a cafeteria at school, but it doesn't look as good as that."

"Whatta ya say?" asked Archie. "Looks kinda good and I'm pretty hungry."

"That makes three of us," said Jim, as he looked for the exit ramp.

When they reached the restaurant, Jim put the top up on the car and looked skyward as he felt a few drops land on his cheek.

"Perfect timing," he said, as the three headed inside.

They were seated at a table and instructed that the food was served cafeteria buffet style with a choice of several hot entrees, sides and desserts.

Jim found the meatloaf that had grabbed his attention on the billboard. Archie had a large scoop of chicken pot pie, and Jimmy had a good helping of lasagna. All three decided it was apple pie or nothing for dessert. As Jim and Archie enjoyed a refill of coffee, Jimmy sat in the corner of their booth with his head leaning toward the corner and let out a long yawn.

"Someone's gonna want to hit the hay soon," said Archie.

It was raining steadily as the guys got back in the Bel Air. Jim unfolded the blanket on the back seat and placed it over Jimmy.

"We're going to make a few more miles tonight, but you can get some sleep if you want, pal. We'll wake you when we pull into a motel."

Jimmy lay back on the large bench that made up the back seat. He loved hearing the rain on the roof and watched the legs of the water gather and run down the back side window of the car. The passing pole lights on the highway illuminated them for seconds at a time at a rhythm which seemed to just weigh heavy on Jimmy's eyes. It wasn't long before he was fast asleep.

The rain continued to come down in buckets as Jim pulled into the motel. After paying for a room, they woke Jimmy and the three made a dash for the door, with Archie shielding the guys most of the way with his Schlitz logo umbrella.

After they dried off a bit, Jim made a few peanut butter and jelly Ritz cracker sandwiches for the three of them.

"Kind of a late night snack tradition of mine," said Jim, as he handed one of the cracker sandwiches to Jimmy, who seemed to be getting his second wind.

"Aa-haa," said Jim, reaching into his old green duffle. "I remember a certain someone asking for a few boxing lessons over the summer."

Jim pulled out an old pair of boxing gloves from his youth. They were a mottled tan in color and stained with years of sweat and leather oil.

Archie looked over at Jim. "Hey, if you sign those, I might be able to sell them in my shop."

"Ha. Fat chance," said Jim, giving Archie the evil eye.

"Here, put these on," said Jim as he tossed them at Jimmy.

"Wow, these are cool," he shot back, tossing the remainder of his peanut butter and jelly cracker in his mouth and quickly slipping his hands into them. They were a bit big for Jimmy, but he didn't mind.

"How do you tie these?" he asked, as he eyed the laces dangling down.

"That's the job of the trainer," said Jim, as he pointed to himself with his thumb. "Hold your arms out straight, one at a time, with your palm facing up."

Jim wrapped the laces around each glove a few times to take up the slack, and then tied the ends of each glove in a bow, like one would tie their shoe.

He then proceeded to show Jimmy the basics of each punch. First jab, then cross, hook and lastly, the uppercut. He then focused solely on the jab, showing Jimmy how to keep his footing for better balance and how to hold his right hand when his left was doing the work.

Jim let him land a few shots as he pretended to become dizzy and fell backwards onto the sofa. Jimmy laughed and moved across the room to Archie, who was busy setting up the checkerboard.

"I can jab, Archie, look!"

Archie turned to look at Jimmy, who thought Archie would be joining in on the mock boxing, too. Before Archie could say, "Wait a minute, Jimmy," a glove landed on his nose and Archie's glasses flew off his face and landed on the checkerboard.

"Oh, my nose!" yelled Archie.

Jimmy's face looked shocked, as he realized Archie wasn't playing. Archie took a Kleenex out of his sweater pocket and dabbed his nose to see if there was any blood, which there wasn't.

"No hitting in checkers, Jimmy," Archie said with a stuffy voice, as he continued to prod his nose in search of blood.

"Sorry, Archie." said Jimmy. "I wasn't trying to beat you up; really I wasn't."

"No, of course not," said Archie.

"Jimmy, we'll do a little more tomorrow. Let's take a break for now," said Jim.

Archie and Jim played checkers for the next few hours, as Jimmy delved into his Captain America comic books he had brought with him, eating his share of the peanut butter and jelly crackers.

"No crumbs in the bed, now," said Jim jokingly.

Jimmy loved the freedom his grandfather had given him. He felt like a big kid, hanging out with Gramps and Archie, staying up past his normal bedtime and taking in the whole experience of being away from home.

When he finished his comic, he jumped back under the covers and pulled them up to his chin as he said goodnight to Gramps and Archie.

It was a comforting feeling as he closed his eyes and nodded off to the sound of two good friends, laughing as they played checkers.

It was around one a.m. when Jimmy woke from his sleep. He could hear Gramps mumbling from his side of the bed.

"Danny... Danny stay a while; don't go. We'll have the weekend together."

Jimmy had grown used to his grandpa talking in his sleep. He had heard it several times over the past few years. Sometimes, it would be just loud enough to wake him and other times it would be loud and shocking as he was awoken.

Sometimes he would hear Gramps get up and wash his face and then get a glass of milk before going back to sleep. He didn't know what exactly Gramps was dreaming, but whenever he did hear a word or two out loud, it was often "Danny," Jimmy's dad.

This time it began soft, but was steadily growing louder.
"Danny... Danny," he shouted again.

This time Jimmy rolled over and rubbed his grandpa's arm.

"Gramps... Gramps... It's me, Jimmy. It's okay. Everything is okay."

Jim stirred in bed and then rolled onto his back. He looked over at Archie, to see if he had woken him up as well, but he was still asleep.

"Jimmy, I must have had a dream. I'm sorry I woke you."
Jim sat up and patted the sweat from his brow with his shirt sleeve.

"It's okay, Gramps," said Jimmy. "I have bad dreams too, sometimes. Mostly about Mrs. Allen's class. Remember the time I thought I had gone to school in my pajamas and everyone was laughing at me."

"Yes, I do," said Jim. "I remember we both went into the kitchen and had cookies and milk before going back to bed."

"What was your dream about?" asked Jimmy.

"Mostly about your dad," replied Jim. "He was my buddy... just like you. We did so much together. I remember in my dream, it was the fourth of July weekend and he was about thirty-two years old. Something like that...
We were about to have dinner. You know, a cookout like we do every year, followed by Archie's fireworks display in the backyard.
Well, Danny kept saying he had to go, and I kept asking him to stay. Eventually he left and I ran out into the front yard as he walked away. He turned to look back once and he smiled and waved to me; but he kept on walking. I guess I just miss him so much. It's hard having your son go before you do. I just wasn't ready for that. I don't think I ever will be."

"I'm sorry, Gramps," said Jimmy, as he rubbed his grandfather's shoulder.

"You don't have to be sorry about anything, pal," said Jim, as he reached over and hugged Jimmy.

"I won't leave you, Gramps. I promise, I'll always be here for you; and when I grow up and get a house someday, you'll come over and have a cookout at my place."

"I'm a lucky guy," said Jim. "I love you, pal."

"I love you too, Gramps."

The next morning, the sun was shining again and the guys hit the road. After a quick gas-up and bathroom stop, they hopped on Route 40 and by late morning, they'd entered the state of Indiana.

Jim decided they should pull off the main route in Richmond and do a little sightseeing. He looked for a McDonald's or a Burger King, as he was having a craving for a juicy burger. That's when he saw the iconic Big Boy statue holding a large cheeseburger on a tray. Being a burger fanatic, Jim had always wanted to try one of these burgers, having seen ads in magazines of the iconic plump, wide-eyed boy, wearing his red and white checkered bib overalls.

He pulled into the parking lot and shouted, "Lunch is on me, boys!"

Jimmy looked up at the huge Big Boy statue.

"Wow, Gramps! This place looks cool!"

"Supposed to have great burgers and strawberry pie, too," answered Jim.

When they sat down at a booth, the waitress dropped off three placemats, napkins and a small package of crayons for Jimmy. Jimmy looked over at Grandpa with a semi-grin.

"I'm a little big to be coloring, Gramps."

"Well, it's part of their job, I guess."

Archie quickly opened the box of crayons and perused through the colors. He grabbed the red crayon and began to color in Big Boy's overalls.

"Then again, some of us never grow up," said Jim with a smile.

Archie didn't look up. He heard Jim's comment but was content to continue coloring. The red and white checkered overalls reminded him of an older checker board he had in the shop back in Philly. Not content with the lone item on Big Boy's tray, Archie drew a can next to the burger and wrote in the word Schlitz on the can.

"Make sure you stay in the lines, Archie," said Jim with a grin.

"When you're my age, staying in the lines is totally optional," said Archie.

"Speaking of our age..." said Jim, "I was thinking we might want to stop in and see Butch when we get to Illinois."

"Butch Carlson?" asked Archie. "Is he still around?"

"He sure is," said Jim. "He wrote me a few months back. He's living in Effingham with his wife, Nancy."

"Who's Butch Carlson?" asked Jimmy.

"He's an old friend of Archie's and mine, from back during the war. A little rough around the edges, but he was a good guy."

"So whatta' ya say, Arch? Let's give him a call and see if he's in. It's on the way, and it's not like we come out this way every year, ya know."

Archie was never keen on reliving that part of his life, but he knew it meant a lot to Jim. After all, it was Butch who pulled Jim's butt off that beach in the Pacific after he was shot. Archie just wasn't the kind of guy to keep in touch with the guys he met in the war. He had known Jim back before he boxed, so that was different.

"Sure, I guess so," said Archie. "At the very least it will break up some of the road travel."

"Great! I'll look him up in the book after lunch and we can give him a call."

They each ordered the double cheeseburger platter, and Archie finished coloring his placemat.

When the trio entered Illinois, the weather was still clear and the air seemed less humid. Soon they would arrive at Butch's place.

Jim had called ahead and Butch had sounded excited to see his old pal.

Seeing a sign for Effingham, Jim turned the Bel Air off the main highway and started down one of the back routes.

The breeze felt good in the back of the convertible as Jimmy lay on his back with his feet propped up near the other end of the bench.
He watched as the clouds came and went from his view. One looked like a large version of George Washington's head, like the one on the side of a quarter. That made him think about his paper route tips. He hoped Michael was doing alright with his deliveries. What if he messed something up, or forgot to deliver them today?

He caught himself worrying and then remembered what Gramps had always told him: "Trust in your family, your friends and the Almighty."
He was pretty sure when Gramps said "Almighty," he meant God.

The head honcho, the big guy upstairs. But Jimmy had always had some doubt about how all that really worked. If God was the head guy in charge, why did his dad die so young? Why did his mom move away? So many hard questions for a nine-year-old.

He had been told his dad was in heaven, and he wondered what they did up there. Did they play checkers like Gramps and Archie did on the green? Did they have music and art? Did they have convertibles, and if so, were there clouds to look at?

If they did have all those things, then why would people have to leave here, just to experience the same stuff somewhere else?

He kept staring up and saw one cloud that looked like a cowboy hat with a feather on the side. He reached into his pocket and took out his Lone Ranger Barlow Pocket Knife, which had a picture of the Lone Ranger and Tonto on the side. He held it up to compare hats, but the cloud had already changed a little and now it looked more like a flattened cap.

He began thinking that when he was bigger, he'd also get a convertible car so he could take his kids cloud watching. That is, when he had kids. Suddenly, Jimmy's cloud watching was interrupted.

"Pull over," shouted Archie.

"You have to go again?" asked Jim.

"No, but there's a ball game goin' on over there and I need to stretch my legs."

Jim could see the game going on near a small school, and within a few minutes had pulled into the parking lot. The only thing Archie loved more than checkers, was baseball. He hopped out of the front seat and grabbed a Schlitz from his cooler. He slickly tucked it into his windbreaker pocket and walked over to the field.

"Well, I guess we're gonna see a ballgame," said Jim.

"Okay with me," said Jimmy.

"Here," said Jim, as he reached into his old, worn leather wallet and handed Jimmy a couple of dollars.

"Thanks, Gramps," said Jimmy, who ran straight over to the field snack shack.

Jim walked over and sat down on the sun-warmed bleacher. He looked over at some of the other spectators who seemed to be mostly family members of the home team, each cheering for their kid, who looked to be around Jimmy's age. They each sat on their own plastic covered cushion or blanket, which seemed like a wise idea, as Jim felt the heat of the bleacher travel through his trouser seat.

The coach started to call out names as they warmed up.

Last names sufficed in this situation, as was traditional with kids sports. Archie stood at his favorite spot, behind home plate, with his fingers between the chain links. He always liked to see the pitches thrown in, pretending he was an umpire making the calls as he watched each one come in.

Archie unassumingly popped open his Schlitz and took a sip. No one seemed to mind, but Jim laughed to himself, as he knew his friend too well. He didn't care if his best bud was a part-time boozer. Archie used to just smoke his pipe, but ever since his wife passed, he drank on a semi-steady basis. It's not that Archie went around drunk. It was more of something to calm his nerves, and Jim accepted him just the way he was.

It was the start of the sixth inning when Jimmy climbed on the bleacher beside Jim; he had a chili dog in one hand and a can of Pepsi in the other, with a pack if baseball cards in his front shirt pocket. The kind that came with chewing gum.

"Are we going to stay for the rest of the game?" asked Jimmy.

"If you want, pal. I know Archie wouldn't mind."

By the time the ninth inning came around, the score was seven to five, with the tying run for the visiting team on second base. There were two outs and the count was one and one.

Archie was rooting for the underdog, and he had already voiced his opinion to the umpire on a bad pitch call earlier in the inning. People in the stands didn't recognize him and thought he might possibly be the grandfather of one of the kids on the visiting team.

Jim simply had lowered his cap slightly during the dispute and avoided eye contact with Archie as he was giving the umpire an earful.

The next pitch was right down the middle; the batter made contact, but popped it up into the stands. Jimmy reached up and caught the ball as it came down, much to the delight of the woman who sat in front of him, who shrieked and covered her head with her hands.

Jimmy looked pleased as he smiled at his grandfather.

"Do I get to keep it?" he asked.

"In Little League you gotta toss it back," said Jim.

As the catcher looked over at the stands, Jimmy tossed the ball back, and the catcher hardly had to move as the ball sailed right to him.

"Nice toss!" said Jim. "We might have to sign you up next year."

The next pitch was a fastball, which sailed past the batter and catcher, smacking Archie on one of his fingers that hung on the chain link fence.

"Aaaaaah... shit!" he yelled.

He instantly cradled his finger with his other hand.

"Son of a bitch!"

The surrounding mothers gasped and gave him the evil eye, after hearing Archie's fine use of the English language.

The umpire just chuckled.

"Sweet justice," he whispered through his mask.

As Archie ran over to the snack shack to get a cup of ice to stick his finger in, Jim looked away, lowering the cap on his head until it almost covered his eyes.

The next pitch was a bit short, and the batter reached with his swing and popped it up over second base. The shortstop was a ball hog and almost ran into the second baseman as he made the game-winning play on the ball.

When Jim and Jimmy walked back to the car, Archie was already in the back seat, holding his finger in the ice and grimacing in pain.

"Whatta' ya say Arch, think we should ask where the local hospital emergency room is?

"Yep," shot back Archie. "Pretty sure it's busted."

After Jim got directions to the local hospital, the three drove off at a good clip.

"Any place else you'd like to stop, Arch? Or should I head straight to the hospital?"

Jim looked into the rear view mirror to see Archie glaring back, lifting his swollen middle finger out of the ice in a not so kind gesture.

Chapter XI

An hour later, Archie was released from the emergency room with a splint on the middle finger of his left hand.

"While you were back with the doc, Arch, I called Butch and told him we'd be a bit delayed," said Jim.

Archie popped open a Schlitz with his good hand and quieted down in the back seat as he enjoyed his beverage.

They arrived at Butch Carlson's house a few hours before sunset. Jim was a little nervous as he rang the doorbell. Many years had passed since he had seen his old friend, and he was never the pen-pal type.

Butch had driven to Philly right after the war ended, and Jim had taken him out on the town. But most of the memories he had of he and Butch were from their days in the Pacific Theater. Those were tight bonds, the kind that are made when you literally place your life in another man's hands. They, and the men in his platoon, had operated as a team. Jim and Butch had been seen as the experienced guys. They had made it through to the end of their tour in Europe, only to be transferred to the Pacific in '44.

They were like older brothers to the newer recruits who had taken the place of men going home. He remembered the exhilarating feeling he had when Germany surrendered, and then how it all changed when his platoon found out how hard it was going to be to get those dug-in Japanese soldiers off those islands in the Pacific.

He had kept thinking he could pick up his boxing career again, and had often fantasized about finally getting his shot at the champ. He was so sure that one day, he'd be defending his own title as champ.

But one bullet had changed all of that. And although his boxing career was lost, it was Butch who helped save his life by literally shielding him with his body and selflessly pulling him off that beach.

Jim waited for the footsteps to come closer to the door, prompting a distant memory he had from the days of collecting money on his paper route. He would often try and guess whether the one opening the door would be male or female by the weight and stride of the steps. He heard nothing. Then the door handle turned.

As the door opened, Jim's gaze shifted from straight across to down, as he saw, for the first time, Butch seated in a wheelchair.

He had an afghan across his lap, but Jim could clearly see that Butch had lost both his legs below the knees. A feeling of awkwardness came over him as he wasn't sure what to say next.

"Hey, Pal!" said Butch. "Come in, come in."

The enthusiasm in his voice was infectious and it immediately lifted Jim's spirits. Jimmy and Archie followed Jim, as they were invited inside. Jim bent down to give his old friend one of his patented bear hugs.

Archie tried not to stare at Butch's lost legs, as he, too, felt a bit awkward. He took his left hand with the broken finger and slowly placed it in his windbreaker pocket. Earlier, he had thought about sharing his mishap with Butch, but now he really didn't feel it was worth bringing up.

Jimmy shook Butch's hand and introduced himself. He noticed the newspaper that was folded and tucked between Butch and the side of the chair with the sports section facing outwards.

"Do you follow baseball, Mr. Carlson?" asked Jimmy.

"You bet, son," replied Butch. I think the Reds are gonna give them Yankees a run for their money this year."

"I'm a Phillies fan," said Jimmy. "Gramps took me to a game last year."

Just then, Butch's wife came into the room with a large smile. She was a very pretty woman and had a touch of silver sprinkled through her shoulder-length auburn hair.

"Hi, I'm Nancy," she said, as she extended her hand to their guests.

"I'm Jim, this is my friend Archie from the old neighborhood back home and my grandson, Jimmy. We're on a cross-country trip during Jimmy's summer break."

"That's wonderful! You just make yourselves at home. I'm going to bring out some snacks for you guys."

Jim, Archie and Jimmy had a seat on the sofa across from Butch, who moved his wheelchair next to a TV tray situated on one side of the room across from their television stand, which also doubled as a bookcase. It held a few baseball and gardening books amid a majority of war history books.

"I know you guys might be asking yourselves, what happened to Butch," he said in an easy voice. "It's okay, I've grown used to initiating the conversation."

"Well, I had decided to make a career of the military and worked my way up to Captain. When we were in Korea, our platoon took a hell of a shelling, and I lost my legs. It was so cold during that first winter, I truly believe the frigid temperature slowed my bleeding and kept me alive until the medics could get to me. I do alright. Nancy still works at the hospital on weekends and I put in some time at the local library. At first it was rough. I went through counseling and a lot of therapy. Just couldn't get over the fact that I made it off that beach in WWII, only to lose my legs a decade later."

Nancy placed some cheese and crackers on a coffee table in front of the guys and another smaller plate on the side table next to Butch. He took her hand in his.

"Nancy and I met during that whole ordeal while I was recuperating in Seoul. She was a nurse with the unit that cared for me. It was love at first sight, you could say."

"It sure was," Nancy answered as she kissed his cheek.

"We'd love for you guys to stay the night if you'd like. We have an extra bedroom and we can set up a cot for Jimmy."

Jim looked over at Archie, who nodded with a smile.
"That would be wonderful. Thank you."

"Not at all," said Nancy. "We'd love the company. It's not every day Butch gets to visit with old friends. How about something to drink?"

"Well, since I won't be driving tonight, a beer would be fine," said Jim. Archie did the same, and Nancy brought Jimmy a cool glass of milk.

"Tell me about yourselves," said Butch. "What have you been up to all these years?"

"Well, like I said on the phone, we're on a sort of road trip."

Jim looked over at Jimmy.

"Hey pal, maybe you'd like to play outside for a bit? Would be good to stretch your legs if you'd like."

"My son Tommy's old bike is in the shed out back if you'd like to ride it," said Butch. He's in North Dakota now, attending flight school. Just watch out for the bee's nest in the back of the shed. As long as you don't bother them, you'll be fine."

"Thanks, Mr. Carlson," said Jimmy, as he went out the front door, milk in hand.

"Be careful," said Jim. "It's going to be dark soon.

Jim looked over at Butch and continued...
"He's a great kid. We're on the road, headed to Las Vegas to try and find his mom. She lit out when he was only four. She left him with my son, Danny. But you know all about what he went through.

"Yeah. So sorry, pal," said Butch.

"I know, we all are. Well, I've been raising him ever since, but I'm not getting any younger, and well, people change, ya know. Maybe it's worth a shot. Maybe not. But for Jimmy's sake we gotta try. We've got a lead that she may be out in Las Vegas. She supposedly cut her first album there, but the record company got bought out, and the new place had her old address; but that's where we'll start."

"Did she make a second record?" asked Butch.

"That's where things get funny. The company said the first record did okay. Not great, but okay. The company said she was working on something that was supposed to have some promise to it. She had sent them the start of one song, and they said it was pretty good. But that's right around when she went missing. They continued to put any royalties into a local bank account she had set up, but there wasn't much to speak of... small change."

"Have you considered the fact that... you know... maybe something happened to her?"

"Sure. Archie and I thought about that possibility. But I have to stay positive for Jimmy's sake. Keep shufflin' forward, you know? Keep your left up, as they say."

"I hear ya, pal. Well, if there's anything I can do, just let me know."

"You're doing it, old friend. You're doing it."

Outside, Jimmy approached the shed with caution. He slowly opened the wooden door, which made a low creaking sound. He could hear some buzzing from the back of the shed. With the late afternoon sun, illuminating part of the back wall, he could see the nest.
"Hornets," he said, under his breath. "Yuck!"

One flew around him curiously, and he noticed that they were drawn to his near-empty milk glass. He drank the rest quickly and then placed the glass down to the right of the shed.

He didn't want to get stung the way Mike Savoy did that summer at Little Joe's birthday party. Mike had left his soda unattended for too long while playing Pin the Tail on the Donkey. When he came back to take a drink, he got stung in his mouth by a hornet.

Mike screamed holy hell, and his mom had to come to pick him up. But Mike did later say that he got a couple of Matchbox cars out of the deal. Parents could often be sympathetic like that.

Inside the door to the left, was a Schwinn Sting Ray. Very much like his back home, only this one was orange. He gently started to pull the bike out, trying not to bang any part of the shed with the handle bars. There were a few spiderwebs on the frame and shifter, but he brushed those off with a broom that was leaning against the shed wall.

Once outside and dusted off, he straddled the top bar and noticed the banana seat was a little bit high for him. He almost went back inside to ask Mr. Carlson for a wrench, so he could adjust the seat, but he was so eager to ride, that he decided to make do.

He pushed off on the pedals as he hopped on the seat. The bike was in second gear, so Jimmy quickly shifted into first. The chain made its familiar clacking sound and the pedaling became smoother. He rode over to the driveway and out into the street, making sure he looked both ways first, as was engrained in his head by his grandpa. He looked over at the picture window in front of the house, for approval in case anyone was watching him through it.

Once on the street, Jimmy shifted into second and picked up speed. He noticed that Tommy didn't have a baseball card mounted to the rear frame, which normally would give the spokes that familiar roaring sound, which was common in his neighborhood back home.

"That made sense," he thought, as Tommy was an older kid and off at college. Maybe when he got home, he'd remove his clothespin and card as well.

As he approached the end of the street, he noticed it veered off to the right and also to the left. He didn't want to go too far, being unfamiliar with the area. The road to the right was a nice downhill stretch, so he decided to press on.

Cresting the hill and starting to head down, he shifted into third so he could gain a little more speed before gliding the remainder of the way. He could feel the wind blowing across his ears as he flew down the hill. Then he noticed a slight wobbling in the front wheel, as the rim looked to be slightly bent.

Approaching the bottom, he was still moving at a fast pace, so he tapped the brakes lightly to slow, but he felt nothing in response. He tried them again, squeezing harder this time and felt the bike only slow slightly. Up ahead was an intersection, and he was now regretting not testing the brakes earlier, as clearly the bike's long stay in the shed had left them needing adjustment.

He felt a nervousness come over him as he desperately wanted to slow the bike down. He tried dragging his sneakers, but the height of the seat only allowed the very tips of his toes to touch, which did nothing to slow him, and only unbalanced him further.

Only yards from the intersection, he frantically squeezed the brakes as hard as he could. The front brake grabbed more substantially than the rear, which caused the bike to shimmy and lurch forward as the front wheel wobbled erratically, causing him to lose control of the steering as he veered off toward the curb. Suddenly, Jimmy was thrown across and over the handle bars, as the bike hit the curb and went down with a crash!

Sounds of a barking dog seemed to get louder in his ears, bringing him back to his surroundings. He wasn't sure how long he had laid there, looking up at the sky, he could tell the sun was starting to set. He knew he was on his back, and he slowly tried to catch his breath. As he struggled to get his bearings, he suddenly noticed that his hands felt like they were on fire. As he held them up in front of his face, he could see sand and small debris covering the parts where the skin had been scraped away by the unyielding asphalt. They bled slightly, so he gently blotted them against the front of his shirt.

"Ow!" he blurted out. More pain arrived.

His senses still not fully awake, he associated the new pain with his right knee. He noticed a large hole torn in his jeans. Jimmy gently felt his knee with his skin-burnt hands.

"Nothing broken," he thought to himself, but noticed that it, too, was scraped badly and bleeding.

"So this was what a wipeout feels like, " he thought. He had heard stories from other kids, but had never experienced one himself until now. He would have altogether abandoned the right of passage if he'd had a choice. Surely nothing to brag about.

Next, he felt his face and teeth, and was glad everything seemed to be okay. He must have tucked his head as he fell. He then noticed a large bump on the back of his head. It was sharply sore to the touch, but didn't seem to be bleeding. He tried to stand and did so, although his head ached even more as he regained his footing.

Looking over at the bike, he noticed the front tire was now flat and the badly bent front wheel was no longer correctly aligned with the handlebars. He lifted the bike up from the street and prepared to walk it up the long hill back to Mr. Carlson's house.

No one had seemed to witness his fall, but he felt humiliated as he held the handle bars at a funny angle, so the front wheel would go in the direction he wanted.

"This is going to be a long, slow walk back," he thought to himself.

Chapter XII

When Jimmy arrived back at the Carlson's house, he rested the damaged bike against the shed. As he walked through the front door, he could see the shocked expression on his grandfather's face.

"What happened to you, Jimmy?"

"I wiped out," said Jimmy. "Sorry, Mr. Carlson. I smashed up Tommy's bike pretty bad."

"Please don't worry about the bike, Jimmy. Let's get you patched up. Nancy, can you come here, please?"

Nancy walked into the room and took one look at Jimmy and said calmly: "Not to worry. We'll get you fixed up as good as new."

She guided Jimmy down the hallway and into the bathroom, where she dampened a wash cloth and gently started to wipe his face, assessing his bumps and scrapes.

She had a gentle way about her that Jimmy really liked. Different than what he was used to with Grandpa and Archie.

She had him change into a pair of Tommy's old shorts so she could attend to his knee. As she had him hold an ice pack on his head, so the bump would go down, she gently cleaned his knee. She then placed some anti-bacterial ointment on it and bandaged it.

"I've treated hundreds of scrapes and bumps in my time as a nurse," she said to Jimmy. "Tommy had his fair share of accidents as well. It's to be expected with boys."

They both giggled a bit. Jimmy really liked the way she looked at him. She had a smile in her eyes that somehow brought back memories of his dad, when he was so young.

It was a feeling that was hard to describe, but maybe something like being wrapped in a warm blanket. Everything was going to be alright. The memories were faint, but none-the-less present. Dancing to music in his dad's arms. The rhythm of the way he spun him around and looked at him.

"I will keep that memory always," he thought.

When she was done, she gave him a gentle hug and walked him back into the living room.

As the guys tried to raise his spirits with talk of how brave he was while intermingling their own stories on spills taken as youngsters, their voices just seemed fade to a whisper, as Jimmy's thoughts turned back to Mrs. Carlson.

"So maybe this is how Mike Savoy felt when his mom picked him up from that birthday party. Maybe this is what it feels like to have a mom," he thought to himself.

As he held the ice pack to his head and listened in on the guys' conversation, Mrs. Carlson brought him a big glass of milk and a plate with three homemade chocolate chip cookies.

"You still got that five and dime store, Archie?" asked Butch.

"It's more of an antique-slash-consignment shop, but yeah, I still have it. Jimmy and his friend Sam were my latest hires for the summer. Good workers, too. They keep me on my toes."

"How many years is that now, twenty-five?"

"Twenty-seven, and it's been an interesting twenty-seven years. Fixed the roof in '58. Had a car slam into the front and break our large window in '71.

"Mr. Bertolini, our neighborhood pizza shop owner, has been trying to expand his shop by inquiring about it for the past decade. I keep turning him down and he comes back to me every year with a higher price. I guess at some point I should give in, but I just love it so. Don't know what I'd do with most of my time otherwise."

"More checkers and ball games," said Jim.

Archie chuckled.

That evening, Butch showed off his new charcoal grill on the back deck of the house. He raved about how charcoal made the best burgers.

No one disagreed with Butch, as they savored the flavor. Jimmy especially loved cheeseburgers and ate every bite. When dinner was finished, Nancy brought out a bowl of coffee ice cream for everyone. Jimmy felt as though the meal had been made in his honor, as coffee was his favorite flavor of ice cream.

"How's your top knot doin', pal?" asked Archie.

"Just fine, Mr. Reynolds," said Jimmy. "The swelling on my head has gone down and my hands feel a lot better, too."

From the back deck, Jimmy could see the Schwinn Stingray, leaning up against the shed.

"Sorry about the bike, Mr. Carlson."

"Nonsense," said Butch. "Don't give it another thought. That old thing hadn't been used for over six or seven years until you rode it. It seemed like Tommy stopped riding it the day after he got his driver's license."

"Ain't that the way," said Jim. "Give a guy the keys to a car and he'll never touch a bicycle for the next several decades."

"Chick magnet," said Archie. "Especially if it's a convertible."

"What's a chick magnet?" asked Jimmy.

Jim stared over at Archie with a grin. "Go ahead; you saddled this bronc…"

Archie took a scoop of coffee ice cream and looked up at the sky as if the right words were going to rain down upon him. Nancy giggled, as did Butch.

"A chick magnet is a… well, it's a type of car… or a type of, uh, thing that attracts women of a specific age."

"Specific age?" asked Nancy.

"Oh, geez. Please don't make this any harder than it is," said Archie.

"Jimmy, it's like when you saw that bicycle in my shop and you were drawn to it. Kind of like a magnet is drawn to metal."

"Oh, so a chick magnet is something that attracts women to metal?"

"No, not metal. More like attracted to, uhh… guys."

"Oh, you mean it makes girls all mushy, like those Partridge family records that have the pictures of the guy with the long hair. I think I understand now, Mr. Reynolds. My friend Sam likes him and says he's handsome."

"There you go, Arch," said Butch. "You don't need a convertible, you just need to grow your hair long."

Jim just about spit out his ice cream, laughing.

That evening, Nancy changed Jimmy's bandages and got him settled in on the cot with a nice blanket and pillow.

"Mr. Carlson said that he got this from the Marines," said Jimmy.

"That's right," said Nancy. "Butch brought this back with several other souvenirs. Comes in handy when we have young guests. Tommy used to sleep on it out here when he was younger. He'd stay up late on Friday nights during the summer, when they would show monster movies until one o'clock in the morning. Most often he'd fall asleep on this cot before they were over and we'd turn the TV off for him."

"Thanks for taking care of me," said Jimmy.

"My pleasure," said Nancy, as she gave him a kiss on the forehead and said goodnight.

The next morning the guys said their goodbyes and Nancy made each of them a sandwich for lunch and a small bag of six golden delicious apples for snacking. Butch brought out his old helmet from WWII and gave it to Jimmy.

"Here ya go, pal. You're in the Marines now, son!"

Jimmy smiled from ear to ear.

"You mean I can have this?"

"You sure can," said Butch. "Tommy never took to it, but I thought you might like it."

"Boy, wait until Mike Savoy sees this, Gramps."

He placed it on his head gently, so as not to get his bump hurting again.

"Wow, it's heavy," said Jimmy.

"Had to be, in war," said Butch. "Plus, it'll keep you safe from overhead birds while you guys are driving in the chick magnet."

Archie laughed and gave Butch and Nancy a handshake, thanking them for their hospitality. Jim gave Butch a bear hug and told him not to be a stranger if he was ever up in Philly again. Archie then took out his Polaroid land camera and they took turns taking different photos. Jimmy requested one of him and Mrs. Carlson. He smiled as he watched the image gradually appear on the square white card.

As the Bel Air convertible pulled out of their driveway, Jimmy waved to Mr. and Mrs. Carlson. His thoughts of their visit, however so short, would stay with him forever.

He sat back with his helmet on and wondered what next awaited him. He looked at the Polaroid picture again, and wondered about his mother.

Chapter XIII

It was a beautiful day, with sunny skies and barely a cloud to be seen as the Bel Air headed out of Illinois and was only a few miles from crossing over the great Mississippi River just north of St. Louis, Missouri.

They had eaten the lunches that Nancy had packed for each of them a few hours ago, and Archie was getting hungry again, remembering the bag of apples she had so generously given them. Jim liked to joke with Archie about his metabolism, and had always said that he was part teenager and part squirrel. Archie always attributed his slender frame to his fast-paced metabolism.

Archie opened the bag and pulled out one of the golden beauties and proceeded to shine it against his shirt. It was tradition to buff a good apple before tasting it.

When Archie bit down into the crispy Golden Delicious, the sound alone instantly made Jim wish to join in.

"Do me a favor, Jimmy," said Jim. Use your pocket knife and slice me a few pieces of apple."

"Don't you want your own, Gramps?" asked Jimmy.

"Yeah, but I can't bite into one of those guys with my bridge, so if you'll just send a few pieces my way, that will work fine."

"Sure thing," said Jimmy, who took out his trusty Roy Rogers and cut off a few generous slabs and passed them forward to Jim.

"How did you lose yours, Gramps?" asked Jimmy.

"Well, it was in June, the year before I went into the Marines, and I was supposed to fight in the Spectrum. Was going against a heavy plodder named Manny Riccardo. He was heavier than me, and could really throw a mean hook. But he was slow, so I could stick and move, picking my openings when I could.
It was in one of the later rounds that he had given me a few good shots and my mouth piece fell out. The ref didn't see it, so we kept boxing, and right after the bell rang to end the round, Manny threw a sucker shot at my face and it landed square on my mouth. It cracked two of my front teeth and loosened a third. Later that week, I had to get the remnants of all three pulled. Then I got that nifty thing. Hated it ever since."

"Did you win the fight?"

"Oh, yeah. I was so mad at Manny, that I dropped him the very next round."

Jim took out his bridge and wrapped it in a napkin, then popped one of the golden delicious slices into his mouth and savored the sweet flavor as he chewed.

"Ya see, this is what happens when you don't brush like you should," said Jim, as he passed the napkin containing his false teeth back to Jimmy.

"Oh, yuck," said Jimmy as he laughed out loud. "That's gross, Gramps."

"And here's what it looks like when you brush daily," said Archie, who smiled at Jimmy like a cheshire cat with his gleaming choppers. "But seriously, your grandpa just wants you to take care of your teeth. But that's not really how he lost his."

Jimmy studied the fake teeth held together by wire. "Maybe I'll be a dentist and make you some better ones," he said.

"Haa. That's okay, kid. You can be whatever you like. You don't have to worry about my theeth," said Jim, lisping.

Jimmy wrapped them back in the napkin and placed it on the bench between Jim and Archie.

When Archie was done with his apple, he wrapped the core in a napkin and placed it in his lap. He handed a napkin back to Jimmy so he could do the same. He then started rummaging through the glove box for anything resembling a small trash bag.

"You really gotta organize this thing," said Archie. "It's a mess."

"It works for me," said Jim.

Jimmy placed his napkin-wrapped core on the front bench next to the other one.

Disgusted with digging through the glovebox and finding nothing to put the garbage in, Archie decided that it would be easier to just toss the cores out the window.

Not being totally sure if Jim would approve, Archie slowly rolled down the side window and rested his arm on the door. Then in one smooth move, grabbed the napkin-wrapped cores and tossed them out.

Jim gave a sharp glare over at Archie. "Did you just do what I 'sink you did?" asked Jim.

"What did he do, Gramps?" asked Jimmy, who was staring out at the Mississippi River.

"Nothing," said Archie.

"Ith's bad enough to lither, but to lie about it... geesh, Arch! Didn't you see that new commercial with the crying Indian brave standing near the highway?"

"Yeah. So?"

"Sooo... sooo?" shouted Jim. "So what do you think he's cryin' about?"

"I dunno," said Archie, with a wise grin on his face. "That fact that we 'thook his land away and built highways?"

"No. The fact that we shouldn't be lithering," said Jim.

"What's lithering?" asked Archie, clearly making fun of Jim's lisp without his bridge in.

Jim didn't answer Archie, he just gave him that "Oh, you're really going to get it" look as he reached on the bench for his teeth.

Grabbing the napkin, Archie opened it and prepared to pop the contents in place, only to discover a wet apple core instead.

"Wha-the heck?!" said Jim. "Okay, thop foolin'. Give me back my theeth!"

Archie looked stunned, like a squirrel not knowing what direction to run in when faced by a speeding car.

"Uh, Jim. I think you better turn around and head back up the highway."

"Why would I want to do that, Arch?"

Archie sunk lower on the bench.

"Because I think I threw your teeth out the window."

"Whaaa!!!" screamed Jim.

Jimmy had never heard his grandpa yell that loud before, and was afraid he might sock Archie.

"That thakes the cake, Arch! That reeeeally thakes the cake!"

Archie just slid closer to the door and shrunk even further down in his seat. Jim didn't say another word as he did a U-turn.

The sun was dipping just below the horizon as Jim gave the old Chevy just enough gas so she could slowly creep along the side of the road. Out in front of the headlights, Archie was stooped over and walking at a slow pace, trying to spot Jim's lost bridge. To anyone driving by, it looked as if Jim was trying to run Archie over, in slow motion.

About ten minutes into his search Archie called out.
"Aaaaa wow!"

"You found something?" yelled Jim.

"No. My damn back went out."

"Well keep looking! We gotha' be close," lisped Jim.

Suddenly, a blue light shown in Jim's rear view mirror. It passed Jim on the left and then pulled over to stop in front of the Bel Air.

An officer got out of his squad car and walked toward Archie, who had just stood up straight and stretched out his sore back.

"What's the problem here, gentlemen?" asked the officer.

"We're looking for a bridge," said Archie.

"Oh, boy," whispered the officer as he rolled his eyes at the thought of seven more hours in his long shift.

"You can't miss it. You know, it's the big one that goes over the Mississippi," answered the officer sarcastically.

"Look, I'm going to need to test you guys for drinking".

"But I'm not driving," answered Archie.

"That's correct," shouted Jim from the Chevy. "I'm driving. We're thrying to find my bridge."

"Okay, then I'll need to test YOU for drinking," said the officer.

"Sit down right there, sir," he said to Archie, motioning to the guard rail near the side of the busy road. The officer then walked up to the car and smiled, citation book in hand.

"Hi," said Jim. "Look, we're sorry, Archie threw my front theeth out the window. We doubled back to thry and find them."

"Why did he do that?" asked the officer, trying not to laugh at Jim's constant lisping.

"He thought they were an apple core."

The officer pointed to a "No Littering" sign, which was only twenty yards from the car.

"Oh, crap," said Jim.

"I'll need to see your license, sir."

Jim handed the officer his license, and hoped Archie didn't cause them to rack up a huge fine for littering. The officer looked over at Jimmy sitting quietly in the back seat and gave him a smile.

"Look Mr. Dillon, I'm gonna let you guys move on, but no more roaming the highways at twilight, and NO littering."

"Yes, sir," said Jim. "Absolutely."

The officer put a few cones out, so traffic on Route 66 would flow around the Bel Air and squad car as the three men looked for Jim's missing teeth.

Luckily, Archie spotted them in the grass. They had apparently flown out of the napkin, but appeared to be undamaged.

The officer stacked up the cones and placed them back in the trunk of the squad car.
"You gentlemen have a good evening, and remember..."

"We know," yelled back Archie. "No more littering. We learned our lesson, officer."

"Learned our lesson?" said Jim, making a face at Archie.

"Get in the car Arch, before I leave you on the side of the road."

Chapter XIV

With the sun going down behind the distant view of the St. Louis Arch, Jim was now feeling pressed to find a motel for the evening. He sped up Route 66, looking for any place nice enough to spend the night, but not overly expensive.

When he saw a roadside billboard for a Howard Johnson's, he sped up to get into the exit lane.

Suddenly, Jim heard a siren and looked up to see a swirling red light attached to a motorcycle in his rearview mirror. "Oh, no!" yelled Jim, "Not again. Doggone it! I was in a hurry to get us some dinner and a room for the night, and lost track of how fast we were going."

"It's not my fault this time. You have a lead foot. I offered to drive," said Archie.

"You? You're not driving! You had too much Schlitz. Just clam up. I'll do the talking. See if you can find the registration in the glove box."

As Jim pulled over to the curb, the motorcycle turned off the siren and pulled up right behind the Bel Air. Jim continued to look in the mirror as the officer put the kickstand down and walked up to the Bel Air with a pad in his hand.

"License and registration please," said the officer.

"Here's my license officer. My friend is looking for the registration."

"Take your time."

"We will," said Archie. "I mean, we'll go slower from now on, officer. You see, I was talking to my friend here about my busted finger and he thinks that I should not stand so close behind the plate, but that's my favorite..."

"Shut up, Arch, and just find the darn registration," snapped Jim.

"I'm trying, but you have a million candy bar wrappers in here. It's amazing you don't have more false teeth."

The officer stared at the license. "Jim Dillon... You aren't Jim Dillon the boxer, are you?"

"He most certainly is," chimed Archie.

"I can speak for myself, Arch, thank you. Yeah, that's me."

"Really... My old man saw you fight. He used to talk about you after reading the paper, too. Said you almost were world heavyweight champ at one point."

"Yeah, almost. I was supposed to be in line for a shot. Then dubya dubya two came and I was drafted. Caught a bullet in my leg in Guam. November of '44 it was. K.O.'ed my boxing career."

"Sorry to hear that. My old man sure was a fan of yours."

Archie started to grow frustrated in his search of the glove box.

"Maybe you'd like to see my pad?" he asked.

"Your whaaat?" said the officer, trying to figure if Archie meant his apartment.

"My pad. Maybe you'd like to see it. It's full of interesting things. It's yellow. Jim wanted me to get white, but they didn't have white. I paid twenty-five for it. Can you believe that?"

"Arch, the registration, please," shouted Jim.

"I was just thinking that since I can't find the registration it would help the situation if the officer saw my pad. "Oh wait, here it is."

Archie handed it to Jim who pulled it sharply from his hand and handed it to the officer.

"He meant his journal pad, officer. He's keeping a record of our travels."

"Oh, okay. I'll be right back fellas; just hold tight."

The officer walked back to his motorcycle and proceeded to call in Jim's plate.

"Would you like to see my pad?" Jim said, trying to mimic Archie's voice. "Really, Arch?"

In a few minutes, the patrolman returned and handed back the license and registration to Jim.

"Everything checks out fine Mr. Dillon. I'm going to give you a warning this time, but keep it slow."

"Will do, officer."

"Thanks officer," said Archie. "Hey, would you like a Schlitz?"

"Uh... no thanks," said the patrolman. "I'm on duty."

Jim slapped his hand on his forehead and rubbed his temples.

"For cryin' out loud, Arch!"

Chapter XV

The next few days ran together for Jimmy. That was the way with summer vacation. He'd often wake up and forget which day of the week it was. But when he thought about it further, those types of details only mattered when they were connected with other things. Like a math test on a Tuesday, or collecting for his newspaper route on Thursdays, or sometimes the occasional drive to church on Sundays.

The three travelers had driven clear through Missouri and were now almost through Oklahoma, and he wasn't quite sure if it was Thursday or Friday, but it didn't really seem to matter. He had a feeling of freedom he had never felt before. He wondered how the early explorers made their way across this country with no roads. It must have been a perilous and marvelous journey all at the same time.

"I bet you know what day it is tomorrow," said Jim.

Jimmy tried to make his best guess... "Friday," he answered.

"No, not the day of the week. There's something pretty special about tomorrow. The twentieth of June."

Suddenly a surprised look came over Jimmy's face. With everything going on, with all the excitement of the trip, he had clearly forgotten his own birthday. He slowly slapped the front of his own face in disbelief.

"It's my tenth birthday!" he shouted.

"That's right, pal," said Jim. "And we're going to make it a special one!"

Jimmy unfolded the road map, which he loved to do first thing in the morning to find where they were, as best he could, by matching locations to highway signs.

The weather was supposed to hit eighty-nine degrees today and Gramps said they'd probably put the top up around lunch time so they wouldn't get too sun burned.

As Jimmy studied the map, he saw an ad on one of the boundaries, which said "Come visit Elk City Lake Park. Elk City, Oklahoma. Camping - Picnicking - Fishing - Swimming."

"Hey Gramps, maybe for my birthday, we can go swimming," said Jimmy.

"I don't think we brought our suits, pal." answered Jim.

Immediately, Jim rethought his quick answer. It was going to be a pretty hot day, and they had been on the road a while without a break.

"Tell you what pal, we're headed through Oklahoma City, keep an eye out for a department store where we could stop and get some bathing suits, and we'll make it happen."

"Cool! Thanks, Gramps!" shouted Jimmy from the back seat. "This is going to be an awesome day!"

The guys found a sporting goods store not far off of the main drag and went inside. There was a large selection of fishing rods off to the right, when they walked inside. It gave Jim a great idea.

"Whatta' you say, we grab a rod and tackle while we're here, pal?" asked Jim, eyeing the sale tags on the rods that were already set up with a reel and line.

"I used to fish at a lake at my grandparents house when I was a kid. I can show you how."

"Sure," said Jimmy. "I heard Billy Ruff tell one of the kids at recess that last summer he caught a huge bass on a Daredevil lure."

Jimmy scanned the lures hung on the wall, looking for the name. He had never seen one before, so he wasn't quite sure what he was looking for. Then he saw it. DAREDEVIL it read in bold letters. It was a red spoon lure with a thick white stripe going down the middle and on the end was a three-pronged hook. In the middle of the white stripe was a picture of the daredevil himself, or at least his face.

"This is it!" shouted Jimmy.

As he looked at the packaging up close, he could see that the face on the lure looked a lot like Ming the Merciless from Flash Gordon, even though he was expecting something more like Evel Knievel.

"Huh," Jimmy said, as he pulled it off the wall hook and handed it to Gramps. "Well, it's supposed to work."

"I'll grab a few bobbers and a package of small hooks, too, in case we want to use night crawlers," said Jim.

"How about you, Mr. Reynolds?" asked Jimmy as he turned around, but Archie was nowhere to be seen."

"Man, he sure is stealthy," said Jimmy.

"Might as well go find him before he finds trouble," said Jim.

On the other side of the store, Archie was looking at the swimming trunks. So many choices and colors.

"A-ha!" he shouted as he pulled his size off of the rack. The suit was a peach color with a white stripe going down each side.

Jim and Jimmy walked up to Arch as he held the trunks in front of him.

"Well, what think, Jimbo?" he asked.

"They make you look like a Creamsicle," said Jim.

"I like 'em," said Archie, as he vanished down another aisle.

Jimmy found a pair that reminded him of Captain America, as they had a red, white and blue theme. Jim went with the conservative navy blue.

As the guys approached the counter with all their gear, Archie ran up with a large box under his left arm.

"What the heck is that?" asked Jim.

"An inflatable boat raft," said Archie. "It was on sale for $1.99"

Jim looked at the packaging, which showed a glamorous model sitting in the bright yellow dingy with pink trim. A soda can sitting in the handy drink holder molded into one side. He looked back at Archie and shook his head, side to side in disapproval.

It was mid-morning on Friday when the guys reached the lake, and they could feel the heat of the day rising. The lake was beautiful, with tall trees lining the bank and a great view of the water as the sun sparkled off the horizon.

"Talk about a view," said Jim, as he found a nice shady spot to park the Bel Air.

Jimmy hopped out and unloaded the fishing gear. Archie pointed out the public bathrooms where the guys proceeded to change into their suits.

When they returned to their spot, Archie unpackaged his raft and began to slowly blow air into the tiny tube on the side. It looked as though he would be there for quite some time, as his cheeks puffed out like a chipmunk in heat.

"Come on," Jim said to Jimmy, "I'll show you how to put a worm on one of these."

They walked out toward the bank of the lake and proceeded to turn over several rocks until they found a few good size worms.

Jimmy made a face in disgust, as Jim placed the bobber on his line and then threaded the hook through the sides of the worm.

"That's gross, Gramps," he said, as the worm wriggled on the hook.

"But still the best way to catch big bass," said Jim. "You'll need to do the same."

"I think I might try my Daredevil lure," Jimmy responded.

"Suit yourself, pal."

Jim showed Jimmy a nice shady spot under some willows, where a large branch had fallen into the water and started to rot.

"That's a good spot," he said, as he cast out in front of the limb. As the bobber and worm made a splash, Jim took up some of the slack in the line and then stuck the butt of his pole in the sand. He kept an eye on the bobber as he walked over to help Jimmy.

"You'll need to be careful with these treble hooks," he told Jimmy. "They are wicked sharp and will catch on anything, including the overhanging branches as well as your skin. So cast carefully. Here, I'll show you."

Jim showed Jimmy how to hold his finger on the string against the pole, as he turned the bail over on the open face reel.

"When you throw out the lure, remove your finger at the same time, so the line can go out. When it hits the water, turn the reel to set the bail and slowly reel in. You can jerk it a few times as you're reeling to make the lure have some life to it. You'll get the hang of it."

The first cast from Jimmy went sky high, and landed only a few feet in front of him, with a splash. He looked surprised at how close it had come to landing on his own head.

His second cast went further, but he had forgotten to set the bail, so when he eventually reeled it in, it had a large hunk of plant on it from the bottom of the lake. He carefully removed it, being sure to stay away from the sharp points.

His third cast was much better. It went about twenty yards and broke the surface of the water smoother. He set the bail and began to slowly reel in, as his grandfather had instructed, tugging every once in a while.

He pictured himself reeling in a monster bass, big enough to feed a small village. His name would be in the paper for catching the Elk City Lake record bass.

Suddenly Jim's bobber began to jump up and down. He ran over to grab his pole from the sand. As his grandfather reeled in the fish, Jimmy watched its tail slap the surface of the water.

As Jim landed the fish, he could see the bright orange belly and large black spot about two inches past its eye.

"A pumpkin seed," he said, slightly disappointed.

"A whaaat?" asked Jimmy.

Jim unhooked the fish and showed Jimmy the roundish pan fish and the black spot which gave the fish its name.

"Are we gonna eat him?" asked Jimmy.

"No, he's an okay size, but we'd need a lot of these to make a meal. We'll throw him back."

"Do you think we'll have fish for lunch?" asked Jimmy.

"I don't know," said Jim. "It's your birthday weekend, what would you like for lunch?"

"I really like it here. Maybe we can get pizza and bring it back here to eat at the picnic tables."

"Perfect idea." said Jim.

Meanwhile, Archie had finished blowing up his one-man boat.

He brought it down to the lake and placed it in the water, admiring his trustworthy vessel. The top was a bright yellow, and the inside and bottom were pink with a yellow rope going around the outside, held in place by a few plastic grommets.

Archie placed a beer in the drink holder and walked into the water.

"Woooo!" he shouted. "Water is still cold."

He proceeded to carefully climb in the small boat. He leaned back into the stern and he pushed off with his feet, floating backwards on the lake. His arms draped over the sides and his feet dangled in the water as his long, skinny legs hung over each side of the bow.

"I dub thee, the S.S. Schlitz!" he shouted as he continued to paddle backwards with his feet.

Jimmy and Jim both laughed at the absurdly bright raft as Archie paddled away.

"Hope you have your sunscreen on," said Jim. "Creamsicles melt pretty fast."

Archie waved back with his left hand, bearing the broken finger.

After an hour of fishing, their luck had only produced a few pan fish. Getting hungry, Jim decided to go grab the pizza as Jimmy had requested. He also was going to surprise Jimmy with a cake if he could find a bakeshop nearby.

"You want to go for the ride?" asked Jim.

"No, I'm gonna keep fishing," said Jimmy, who was perfecting his cast with the Daredevil lure."

"O.K., I'll be back in a little while. Pepperoni and sausage, right?"

"Right!" answered Jimmy.

The wind started to pick up a bit as a few clouds drifted in from the west. Suddenly, Jimmy had what felt like a bite on his lure. His excitement grew as he felt it again and gave a great tug on the pole.

To his surprise, out shot the lure from the water, and came racing back at him. He closed his eyes as for that split moment he felt helpless. He must have yanked the lure out before the hook was set.

The Daredevil went flying past his head and landed in a nearby shrub behind him.

"Crap!" shouted Jimmy.

He then looked around to see if anyone heard him swear at his unfortunate situation. No one seemed to be close by, and Archie, who had finished his Schlitz, looked to be asleep out in his small boat.

Jimmy hurried to get the lure untangled from the shrub and luckily it wasn't wound too badly. He quickly reeled in the excess line and removed the lure from its trap.

"Gotta be quick," he thought. "That fish might still be there!"

He pulled the rod back over his shoulder and prepared for a mighty cast. Releasing his finger from the line, he let the pole fly forward. Out went the daredevil and line with a whizz.
It was, in fact, a great cast; a cast that would have gone thirty yards easy, had it not been for the wind gust that blew the lure over to the right, where it landing with a "thwap!"

Jimmy looked for the splash in the water but couldn't see where the lure landed at first. Then he closed the bail and proceed to reel in the line, following the sight of the thin white filament, until he saw where it had landed... smack on the back of Archie's raft.

"Crap," he said again, only this time, under his breath.

He tugged gently on the line, but the lure did not give.

He then moved the rod tip side to side in a whipping motion, to see if that would free the lure. But no such luck.

Archie was still not aware of the situation as Jimmy gave one last hefty tug backwards.

Off tore the lure, as it flew back toward Jimmy, who luckily sidestepped its approach as it landed beside him in the sand.

Attached to the treble hook was a small piece of yellow vinyl. The daredevil face looked back at Jimmy with that sly grin.

"Oh, crap," Jimmy said again to himself. "Maybe Archie won't notice."

Jimmy tore the yellow vinyl piece off his hook and tucked it into the side pocket of his trunks.

The wind continued to blow Archie to the right, away from the spot they had staked out, and further down the lake. Still thirty or so yards out from shore, the bright yellow and pink vessel with its single passenger, appeared in front of a family that was at the next picnic site down from theirs.

It was the cool water touching the back of Archie's neck that woke him from his slumber. His legs also seemed to sitting deeper in the water.

Suddenly he was wide awake. He wasn't the best swimmer, and a panicked look came over his face as he searched for the reason his boat was leaking. As he turned his head to the left, he could see the small hole about the size of a nickel, and could hear the air whooshing out. He tried to reach over with his other hand and pinch the hole shut, but his wrapped finger made the use of the hand clumsy.

Lower still, he sank in the water, as his butt was now sinking low in the boat and much lower into the water. He tried to kick to generate some momentum, but that just seemed to make matters worse as more air escaped.

The family on shore, enjoying their picnic lunch, was bewildered by the goofball flopping around on his sinking boat.

With the S.S. Schlitz now barely resembling a boat, Archie knew he had to flip onto his belly and use the remaining air in his raft to get to shore. As he flopped over, he struggled to kick with his feet and started using his hands in some sort of hybrid dog paddle, although it wasn't working all that well with his busted finger.

To the family on shore, he looked like one of those splashing wildebeests from Marlin Perkins' Wild Kingdom, getting attacked by a crocodile.

"What is that man doing?" the little girl asked her dad.

"I don't know honey, maybe he has a cramp," he answered.

"Maybe he's gotta go pee," said her bother, laughing.

"Abandon ship!" yelled Archie, as he freed himself from the vinyl amoeba and continued trying to dog paddle to shore.

The dad on shore finally stood up and walked down to the bank of the lake.

"Stand up!" he shouted. "Stand up!

Archie did as he was told and stood up. He noticed to his embarrassment, the water only came up just past his waist.

Grabbing the rope from his raft, he dragged it, along with the empty Schlitz can, which was still in its holder, onto the beach and down the sandy bank, back toward Jimmy.

Chapter XVI

When Jim returned with the pizza, he could clearly see Archie had gotten his fair share of sun. Along with the pizza, Jim had brought back a small box cake and ten small candles for the top. He placed the box down beside him on the picnic table seat, in hopes of surprising Jimmy.

"Man, Arch," said Jim. "We're having pizza not lobster. They do make sun screen ya know."

"I know. Sun felt so good, I ended up falling asleep. Woke up when my boat popped."

"Yeah, those cheap inflatable boats will let you down every time. I bet that shower ought to feel really good tonight," said Jim sarcastically.

Archie just shot him back a wise grin.

"Pepperoni and sausage has arrived!" Jim shouted to his grandson.

Jimmy quickly reeled in his fishing line and ran back to the picnic table under the shade of the tall willows.

"I'm starved," said Archie, whose red arms and neck were in stark contrast to his white tee shirt.

Jim served up the pizza and the three joked about Archie's boating mishap as they ate. Archie was sure it was a defective seam, and Jimmy smiled to himself not letting on what or who the real culprit was.

When the pizza was finished, Jim lifted up the small box cake. German Chocolate, it said on the side.

"Hey, you got my favorite," said Jimmy.

"I went in looking, not sure what selection they'd have, and there it was," said Jim. "In the same aisle as the ice cream."

Jim placed the candles on the cake and Archie lit them all with his Bic lighter.

"Gotta hand it to them Germans," said Archie. "When it comes to chocolate desserts, they take the cake. Make a wish, kid," said Archie, as he lit the last candle.

Jimmy closed his eyes tight and hesitated for a few moments in deep thought. Then opened them and blew out all ten in one mighty puff.

"What did you wish for?" asked Archie.

"Oh, Mr. Reynolds, you know that you can't tell what you wish for, or it won't come true."

"Maybe he wished you up a new inflatable boat," joked Jim.

As the guys ate the birthday cake, Jimmy thought about his wish. It wasn't much like his past wishes. No Matchbox or Hot Wheels cars. No new baseball glove, comic books or G.I. Joe toys. In fact, it wasn't a material thing at all. It was more of an idea.

"Maybe that's what growing up is all about," he thought. Maybe there was a more important wish. After all, he was now in the double digits. That in-between stage between single digits and becoming a teenager. He was proud of his wish, and he wanted in the worst way to tell Gramps, as he knew he'd be proud of him. But he truly believed that in order for the wish to come true, he had to keep it a secret.

Jim had one more surprise for Jimmy, as he pulled out a thin paper bag from under the picnic table.

"This is from Archie and me," said Jim.

Jimmy opened the bag and gave a big smile, as he pulled out a stack of eight comic books from the bag. It was the Captain America Tales of Suspense origin story series.

"Wow, thanks guys!" shouted Jimmy.

"Those issues were printed in 1965," said Archie. "The same year you were born."

"That's right," said Jim. "Archie and I saw those come into his shop a few months back while we were talking baseball and eating a few doughnuts. As soon as I saw them, I asked him to tuck them away."

Jimmy opened the first book in the series and flipped through the pages, which released the all too familiar comic book odor of archived paper and ink. Not wanting to risk getting any frosting on the pages, he popped them back into their protective bag and gave his grandpa and Archie a hug.

That evening in their motel room, after Jimmy had brushed his teeth, he sat in bed, close to the lamp light with his pillow behind his back, reading the amazing story of the Captain America origin.

"This truly was a special birthday," he thought. He just didn't want the day to end.

When Jimmy finished the first issue in the series, he closed it and placed it on the nightstand next to him. He thought again about his special wish, and how he didn't even have to wish for the comics. It was as if wishing for the right thing somehow made everything else fall into place.

He then said goodnight to Jim and Archie, said all his prayers and thanked them both for a great birthday and then drifted off to sleep, content with knowing he was now a decade old, and that he was loved.

Chapter XVII

It was a rainy Tuesday afternoon when Archie asked to stop at a local Western Clothing shop he spotted on one of the back roads of the small town of Groom, Texas. It was his personal mission to get a cowboy hat.

Archie had spoken to a few people when gassing up at local service stations after they had entered Oklahoma, and saw that most of the men wore some type of western hat.

"When in Rome...," he said to Jim.

"You mean, when in Texas," replied Jim, with a drawl.

Jimmy was pretty keen on the idea, too, as he had been a big fan of western TV shows like Bonanza and Gunsmoke.

Archie began trying several of them on, searching for one he liked best. The large brim hats were just too big for his slight frame and narrow face. He even tried on a bowler, but thought he looked too much like a banker and not the free-spirit look he was going for.

Meanwhile, Jim tried on a nice 10x beaver fur felt Stetson hat with a nice wide brim and a front-pinched crown. He looked at himself in the mirror and was not sure if it was good or bad, until Jimmy spoke up.

"You kind of look like John Wayne, Gramps," said Jimmy.

"Yah, you do kinda look like the Duke," said Archie, as he continued to try on different hats, still not pleased with what he was finding.

Jim took one look at the price and then gently put the hat back on the rack. Sixty-five dollars was probably O.K. for the Duke, but too rich for his blood, even if the hat did contain genuine beaver fur felt. He placed his short-brimmed wool driver's cap back on his head and nodded in approval of his decision.

Jimmy started to look around the store and found a display of silver-colored sheriff badges with each featuring a different name on the front. He spun the display around slowly, looking through the names in alphabetical order until he came across one that said JIM.
He temporarily took the badge off the rack and pinned it to his shirt. He then took a bandana from a nearby rack and tied it around his face so it covered his nose and mouth. Lastly, he placed one of the cowboy hats on his head. It was a little big, but it still completed his outfit.

"Stick-em up," he said to Archie, as he came up behind him and pointed a finger in his back.

Archie quickly put his hands in the air.
"Please Mr. Bandit, I give up," he said in a high-pitched voice.

"This is a great disguise. Bet you didn't know it was me, did ya Mr. Reynolds," said Jimmy.

"Oh, it's great," said Archie. "Only I don't think bandits who wore their name on the front of their shirts got away with many hold-ups."

Jimmy laughed and placed the items back where he had found them. Archie finally found a hat he thought was right. It was more of a western looking fedora, than a true cowboy hat, but it looked good on his head. It was light tan in color with a sharp looking brown, silk hatband going around the crown.

"Not bad, Arch," said Jim. "You look like a western Humphrey Bogart."

"I was thinking more like Jason Robards," said Archie.

Jimmy had found another display with a mannequin, dressed as a cowboy with a leather vest, Stetson hat, cowboy boots and gun belt, which held a replica six-shooter.

"Wow, that is cool!" said Jimmy.

A large man with a thick mustache who stood nearby, could see the excitement on Jimmy's face and decided to share a little history about cowboys. He told Jimmy that while the owner thought it made an attractive display, most real cowboys never carried six-shooters.

"Really?" asked Jimmy. "But everyone on Bonanza carries a six-shooter."

"Well, a single action revolver back then would cost a cowboy roughly two weeks pay," said the man. "And they just weren't really practical. Most cowboys carried a rifle in a scabbard on their horse. It was much more accurate due to the longer sight plane, and it could put food on the table much better than any revolver."

"You mean they would rather have a rifle, than a six-shooter?"

"Yep," said the man. "That would be their choice every day of the week and twice on Sundays. The revolver came out of the military, as it was first introduced for the calvary, so they could hold the reins of their horse in one hand and fire their revolver with the other. The barrels on those guns were over seven inches long. But outside of the military, they just weren't as popular. Some men felt the need to own one, but most guys couldn't hit the broad side of a barn with it."

Jimmy cocked his head in confusion, as he tried to picture a man shooting at the side of a barn and missing entirely.

"Wow. I never knew that. I guess if I was a cowboy, I'd choose the rifle, too."

"Wise choice," said the man.

He walked over to a display that had many different colors of bandanas. He had noticed Jimmy wearing the red one earlier. He took that one from the shelf and handed it to Jimmy.

"Here," said the man, as he handed it to Jimmy. "My gift."

"Wow, thanks!" said Jimmy.

He took a minute to look at the red bandana that had many different cattle brands printed on it as a design. He then tied it behind him and wore it around his neck.

"You look good," said the man. "Just like a real cowboy. You know those came in real handy because they had so many uses."

"Like what?" asked Jimmy.

"Well, for instance, cowboys would use it to block out the trail dust from their nose and mouth. But they would also use it to wipe the sweat from the inside of their hatband, or fold it to use as a pot holder when removing a hot dinner pot from the campfire, or use it to soak up water from a nearly-dry creek bed and then wring out the water back into a canteen. You could even fold it thin and use it as a bandage in a real pinch."

"Thanks, Mister. I really like it."

"My name's Ray," said the man, as he offered his hand to Jimmy.

Jimmy gave the man a tight hand shake, just like his grandpa had taught him.

"You've got a good grip, partner," said Ray. "It was a pleasure talking to you."

"You too, sir," said Jimmy.

Archie brought his hat of choice to the front counter and paid for it. He snugged down the fedora on his head so it wouldn't go flying from the convertible, as they drove further west toward Amarillo.

As they drove down the highway, Jim saw a billboard for the Cadillac Ranch. It was an art sculpture of ten Cadillacs from various years, planted into the ground so their tail fins stood up toward the sky at an angle.

"Let's check this place out," said Jim. "I actually read an article in Reader's Digest about this place. Some group of artists had money from a benefactor and planted these cars in the ground as artwork. They supposedly buried them in order from oldest to newest."

"Wow! I can't image having enough money to just stick a car in the ground," said Archie.

As the guys drove along the scenic highway, there in front of them appeared the sculptures, stuck in the ground in the middle of nowhere, as if they all fell from the sky, or grew up from the ground.

Jim pulled safely off the road and shut off the Bel Air. He patted his car on the dashboard.

"There, there, ol' girl. No one is gonna bury you in the ground, I promise."

The guys got out and started wandering down the row of cars. It was amazing how everything lined up: the spacing to the cars, the angle in which they were buried, and how the depth of each of them was exact. Jim, being a car buff, named off the years as they walked past them.

"This first one is a '49," he said. I can tell by the fins and back lights."

Each car was buried up to its hood, with the front windshield in the ground and the remainder of the car sticking up at an angle. Jimmy crawled into one of the cars through its side window, and Archie took his picture with the Polaroid camera.

"This is so cool," he said, as he disappeared through one door and reappeared out the other.

As they walked toward the back of the row, which featured the later sixties models, the sky started to grow dark.

"Looks like we might get a bit of rain," said Jim, who was too enamored with the sculptures to cut their tour short because of a few clouds.

"Rain is okay with me," said Archie. "I can put my new hat to the test."

By the time they reached the last car, the sky was an eerie sort of greenish grey and the wind had started to pick up.

"We best head back to the Chevy," said Jim. "That sky is looking ominous."

As they started to walk back to their car, which was roughly a hundred yards away, something made a pinging sound off one of the cars.

At first Jim thought Jimmy might be fooling around by tossing a small rock, but then he heard another and another. The sound came more rapidly.

"It's hail!" he shouted. "Head to the car, quick!"

Soon hundreds of hail stones about the size of grapes started to fall from the sky. Jim quickly grabbed Jimmy and pulled him in close, so he could lean over him and shield him from the stones with his arms.

"Ouch!," said Archie, as one hit him on the shoulder as he ran, and then another struck his arm. "Damn it!" he yelled.

Jim was feeling the stones hit his back as he leaned forward and shuffled on quickly. Some hit his head too, but his cap helped absorb most of the sting. Soon they were at their car, and Jim felt it would take too long to get the top up.

"Quick, get under the car," he said.

All three guys squeezed tightly under the car's frame as they heard the increasing frequency of hail stones hitting the windshield and hood of the car. In a few minutes it was over, and Jim gave the all-clear to crawl out from under the Chevy.

When they stood up, they could see thousands of stones all around them, covering the road as well as the surrounding farmland. The ones on the hot ground started to melt immediately. Jimmy picked one of the stones up and studied the small jagged piece of ice in his hand.

As Jim walked around to the front of his car, he noticed that the windshield was cracked in two places.

"Oh, no," he said. "I can't believe this. He looked at the hood as well, and could only see one or two small dents, where the rest of the hood looked to be undamaged.

"I should probably get this windshield replaced," he said. "But it'll have to wait for now. We'll see if there is a service station up ahead somewhere."

Archie climbed into the convertible and started tossing out all the stones that had fallen inside the car. Jimmy helped as well.

"I've never seen anything like that before," said Jim.

"Me neither," said Jimmy.

"You got some welts on the back of your neck," said Archie to Jim.

"I'm fine," he responded. "I don't think any of them broke the skin. Good thing we had our hats though, or each of us would have one heck of a headache."

As they drove into downtown Amarillo, Jim pulled into a service station to see about the windshield. A man Jim's age came out and shook his hand.

"Hi, I'm Ben Herford, station owner. What can I do for y'all?"

'Well, we got caught in that hail storm this afternoon and our windshield is pretty cracked up. Would you happen to have a replacement?"

"Might be," said Ben. "I got a cousin Henry, just up the road a piece in Tascosa. He owns a salvage yard and has hundreds of old cars. Probably has a '57 windshield. Let me give him a call."

Jim grabbed a soda pop for himself and Jimmy as they waited for Ben to return. Archie had just finished a Schlitz and was in the service station bathroom.

In just a few minutes, Ben came back, all smiles.

"Woo-wee, your lucky day. He's got a '57 alright. Says he'll sell it to you for twenty-five dollars, but will install it for you for thirty."

"Seems like a good deal," said Jim.

Ben gave Jim directions to his cousin's place in Tascosa, which turned out to be only forty minutes away.

It would be kind to say Ben's cousin Henry was disorganized, but the truth be told, Henry was a hoarder. When Jim, Archie and Jimmy walked into his office (if you could call it that), which was attached to his warehouse, you could not see the desk, because it was covered with random receipts, greasy auto parts odds and ends, and binders that contained mostly parts manuals, but also a few dog-eared Playboy magazines.

The rest of the office had stacked boxes, more random parts and a phone that hung on the wall, which looked to at one time have been light blue in color.

"Ben told me y'all be comin'," said Henry in a thick drawl. I kin install it for ya', if yer fixin to pay in cash."

"Yessir, we're fixin to pay in cash," said Jim.

"Then just make yerself at home. Pop machine in the corner there, and I'll git right to it. Feel free to explore the yard if y'all see fit. Gonna take me 'bout two hours."

Henry took the keys from Jim and drove the Chevy up to the garage and into one of two garage bays. The second bay was filled with junked parts.

Jim was a little nervous handing over his baby to someone whose English he could barely understand, but figured he had few options at this point. He then looked over at an old couch, which was covered in a gray flannel sheet. It seemed to be the only place to sit down in the shop, and it was mostly covered in dog hair. An old German shepherd lay idle on one side. The dog followed Henry around with his eyes, but didn't move a muscle, as it seemed content with the sun coming in through the only window, warming its coat.

"I don't know about you guys," said Jim, "But I think I'll explore the junkyard."

"Agreed," said Archie, who didn't relish staying inside with the dog. He followed Jim and Jimmy outside.

The junkyard seemed to go on forever. It wasn't like the junkyards back east that Jim had visited for parts now and then. Those were well managed with rows of cars. Each of which was neatly stacked four or five high and sorted by make and model.

Henry's idea of a junkyard was to tow the car into the field with a tractor and let nature grow up around it. There was no rhyme or reason to any specific model, or condition. Some cars were stacked, while others weren't. There were no rows, and cars were distributed more like a random maze. One car, an old olive green Oldsmobile, was upside down on its roof, with its exhaust system removed.

"A guy could get lost out here," said Jim. Although he could clearly see the joy on Jimmy's face as he looked eager to explore the maze of rusty gold.

"Go ahead and look around," said Jim. "Just check back in with Archie or me once in a while. Oh, and watch out for snakes. This is Texas, after all."

"I'll be safe," said Jimmy, who ran off toward an old John Deere tractor that had wheels as tall as him. The tractor had a high seat and when Jimmy climbed aboard, he had a great vantage point to other areas of the yard.

What caught his eye in the distance, was what looked to be an old motorcycle, with large red fenders and a shifter similar to his Schwinn Stingray back home. He ran over to the motorcycle and ran his hand over the old paint. It was a real beauty and had the face of an Indian on the gas tank. The kickstand looked to be firmly in place, so he climbed up onto the seat and grabbed the handle bars.

He had to really stretch to reach them, but the feeling of being on the bike was exciting.

He made a rumble with his voice as he pretended to shift from gear to gear while cruising down the highway.

As he shook the handle bars and bounced on the seat, he began to hear a buzzing sound that seemed to come from under the front of the bike.

Meanwhile, closer to the barn, Archie had climbed into an old, rusted red Ford pickup truck. It was missing the front two headlights, but the signature thick grill wall was still in place, as were the whitewall tires, even though they were flat. He adjusted the rearview mirror and pretended to shift and drive the old truck.

"I've wanted one of these ever since I started watching Sanford and Son," said Archie. "I could picture myself touring the countryside in search of antiques for the shop. I wonder how much it would take to get it running?"

When Jim opened the front hood, he was shocked to see the engine compartment completely vacant. Only a bunch of weeds were growing up from the opening.

"I don't think this one will be running anytime soon, buddy," joked Jim.

Suddenly, Jim could hear Jimmy yelling in the distance.

"Wonder what he's up to?" asked Archie.

Archie could see Jimmy in the truck's rearview mirror, running through the weeds toward them as fast as he could, while waving his arms frantically in the air.

"Uh-oh," said Archie, who closed the front door and rolled up the side window. "Get in quick!"

As Jimmy got close to to the truck, Jim could see he wasn't slowing down.

"Hornets!" Jimmy yelled, as he ran right past the truck and kept going.

"Oh, hell!" yelled Jim. "This ain't gonna be pretty."

"He's already doing it," said Archie. "Just gotta run until you're out of their territory. Remember that time you and I got stung."

"Yeah, but it was mostly you. I think I outran you," said Jim.

Archie and Jim stayed frozen in the Ford truck, watching safely from behind the windshield until the coast was clear.

A few minutes later, it was all over. Jim and Archie walked around to the front of the shop, where Jimmy was sitting on the concrete front stoop with his shirt off, while Henry's wife had gone inside to get some of her famous hornet paste, made from baking soda and water.

Happens 'bout once a year ta' me," Henry said to Jimmy, in an effort to make him feel better. "Yella' bastards sting like hell," he added.

Jimmy stepped on his shirt a few times in anger to get retribution on the hornets that were still crawling inside.

Henry's wife then appeared with a coffee mug in hand and proceeded to rub her remedy paste onto Jimmy's stings.

"Good thing about those hornets, is they don't leave their stingers in ya'," she said. "This will ease the pain and swelling."

After she was done attending to Jimmy's stings, which totaled eight, she brought him a black cherry soda pop.

"Oww, it hurts so much," said Jimmy, as he winced. "Can't believe hail and hornets all in the same day."

The black cherry soda somehow tasted more flavorful and rewarding, as he did his best to fight off the pain of the awful, throbbing stings.

"Will make a good story to write to your friend Sam about," said Jim. "We can grab a postcard at the motel tonight."

"You're being pretty brave," said Archie. "And you did the right thing by running out of the area."

"I was sitting on an old motorcycle, when I heard buzzing," he said. "It must have been their nest in the ground."

"I reckon so, boy," said Henry, who mussed Jimmy's hair in a friendly manner and then walked back into the garage to continue his work.

It took Henry a full two hours to fix the windshield. By then, Jim had fallen asleep on the couch next to the German shepherd, who had moved his head onto Jim's thigh. Archie was relaxed, puffing on his pipe while he thoroughly perused through both Playboys.

When Henry backed the Bel Air out of the garage, it looked as good as it had in years.

"Wow," said Jim. "It looks as good as new. You even got the dents out of the hood!"

"Yah, I've always had a knack fer fixin' dents," said Henry.

"Lousy housekeeper, but good as hell on body work," whispered Archie to Jim.

Jim paid Henry as promised, and the guys were soon on their way to New Mexico. As they drove down the highway, the windscreen gave a much clearer and more rewarding view of the glowing orange and purple sun, as it slowly started to make its way lower in the western sky.

Chapter XVIII

It was upon reaching Albuquerque that Jim decided to gas up at a Texaco station and clean their new windscreen, which had accumulated a few bugs from the highway. The station looked to have restrooms as well as a small store.

"Can I gas it up?" asked Jimmy, as they pulled up to the pump.

"Sure," said Jim, but let's hit the john first. It might be a while before we see another station, so I suggest everyone go while we're here. You catch that, Arch?"

"Yeah, yeah. I'll go, but first I'm going to pick out a snack," said Archie, as he walked toward the station entrance.

No sooner had Jim and Jimmy walked away from the car, when a large delivery box truck pulled into the station.

A heavy-set driver jumped out of the cab, looking to be in a hurry, as he got out and ran around to the rear of the truck, where he unlatched the back door of his trailer.

Lifting the door with his arms above his head, he gave the door a shove and it shot open on its track of rollers. As soon as it had opened, it started to roll back shut.

"Damn door," said the driver, as he pushed it open again, "They over-greased the track again!"

He made sure to push a second time so the door stayed up. The driver looked inside, inspecting his cargo.

"Damn!" he shouted again. "The stupid A/C unit is on the fritz again. It's gonna get hotter than H-E double hockey sticks in here if I don't come up with a fix."

The driver ran inside the station with much haste, unintentionally cutting in front of Archie, who was about to step up to the counter with his bag of beef jerky and a pack of peppermint Tic-Tacs.

"How much ice do you have in your cooler?" the driver asked the cashier, as he tried to catch his breath.

"We have a delivery coming next week; but the cooler should at least be half-full. If you can wait a second, I'll check," answered the cashier.

She walked out to the cooler and came back a minute later.
"I've got twenty-two bags."

"I'll take 'em all." said the driver. "I've got fifty-two cases of Schlitz I'm delivering to Las Vegas and my fridge unit went out thirty miles back."

Archie's ears perked up as he heard the brand name of his favorite beverage.

"I can help you load that ice, mister," said Archie as he paid for his items and quickly followed the driver out the door.

The way Archie saw it, playing the good samaritan couldn't hurt, especially if the driver saw fit to give Archie a small, icy-cool reward. The driver looked at Archie's thin build with his red short sleeve oxford, tan slacks and loafers, then at his busted finger.

"I don't mind the help," said the driver, "but are you sure you're okay to be doing that kind of work?"

"My good man, I grew up on a farm before moving to the city. I'd be glad to give a hand. Name's Archie Reynolds," he said, as he offered his hand.

"Ben Jaworski," said the driver, as he gave Archie a firm shake.

Ben pulled his truck around to the side of the building where the ice chest was located.

"I'll climb up in the truck, and you can toss me up those bags one at a time," said Ben.

"Sounds like a plan," said Archie.

The bags of ice were heavier than Archie had anticipated, and as he swung the first bag upward, it hit the edge of the trailer frame and broke clean open, showering the small cubes all over the inside floor of the trailer.

"Oops," said Archie. "Sorry, must have miscalculated that one."

As Archie tossed up each of the remaining ten-pound bags of ice, Ben would walk each one back into the trailer and place it on top of the cardboard boxes which held the beer, working from back to front.

In just a few minutes, the two men had placed all twenty-two bags in the trailer.

"Well, that ought to keep her cool for a while," said Ben. "Tell ya what, I gotta go relieve me of a chili dog I had at lunch. Why don't you help yourself to a six-pack? Just close the door when you're done, so it stays cool in there. This chili dog is tellin' me I might be a while."

"Thanks," said Archie, who wore a huge grin on his face. He quickly ran back to the car to retrieve his canvas tote bag. He removed the checkers and his umbrella to make room for his new gift.

Archie ran back to the truck and climbed up inside. He then walked to the front of the trailer. It was hot as heck outside and it felt good to take a minute and enjoy the cool, shady oasis of the box truck. He pulled open one of the cardboard boxes, and helped himself to one of the six packs of cool Schlitz.

Before placing the beer in his tote, Archie pressed the six pack to his forehead, exuding a long sigh and anticipated enjoying his prize in the fifty-six convertible. As he turned to walk out of the trailer, Archie slipped on one of the stray ice cubes that covered the trailer floor. Reaching for anything to regain his balance, he grabbed at the upper door lip, which only made matters worse, as it pushed forward on its slick track. Archie's feet flew up as ice shot out from under his loafers. His head came down on the floor of the trailer with a thump. The door continued to move forward until the momentum caused it to come down hard, tripping the outside door latch as it shut with a bang.

Meanwhile, Ben Jaworski, who was walking quickly like a man on a mission, passed Jim and Jimmy, who had just walked out of the service station bathroom.

As they came around the corner, Jim looked at the empty Chevy.

"Huh, Archie must still be inside. Here, I'll show you how to gas her up," said Jim. "Then we can grab a snack and hit the road."

Jimmy watched as the numbers revolved on the pump dial. They came to a stop at fourteen gallons.

"It says eight dollars and twenty-six cents, Gramps," yelled Jimmy.

Jim, who was waiting in the front seat, pulled a twenty dollar bill from his wallet and gave it to Jimmy so he could pay the attendant.

"Used to be gasoline was cheap," said Jim. "Here, use the change to get yourself something. Oh, and if you see Archie, please tell him that the bus is leaving."

Jimmy thanked his grandpa, ran inside and came back a few minutes later with a bag of chips and a Coke.

"I didn't see him inside," said Jimmy.

"Huh, I'll go look in the john. Stay in the car, Jimmy."

While Jim was walking around the back of the station to the bathroom, a large delivery box truck pulled out of the station from the opposite side and headed west down the highway.

Jim knocked on the bathroom door and got no reply. He opened it up to take a look inside, but didn't see Archie.

"Woooo," he said. "Someone oughta spray in here."

Jim then walked inside the station and up to the cashier.

"Excuse me, did you see a guy in his sixties come in here, wearing a red short sleeve shirt and tan slacks?"

"Yeah," said the girl. "He bought a couple of things and walked out with some truck driver. Said something about helping him load a bunch of ice so he could keep his beer cold."

"Do you remember what kind of truck it was?"

"It was one of those large delivery trucks, you know, with the big box trailer on the back. I think he said he was hauling Schlitz."

"Oh, crap," said Jim under his breath. How could Archie do that to him and Jimmy? He knows how important this trip is.

"Him and his damn Schlitz!" he swore.

Jim jumped back in the Chevy and told Jimmy he could ride up front with him.

"Really?" asked Jimmy, "I thought Archie got sick when he rode in the back seat."

"He does," said Jim. "But Archie just rode off with a truck driver. I just can't believe it!" added Jim, fuming as he clutched the steering wheel.

"That nincompoop! He probably thinks this is a funny joke."

"You mean, he's really gone?" asked Jimmy.

Jim just shook his head in disappointment.

"Just wait until we catch up with him. Just wait! Knowing Archie's yap, he'll be dropped off at the driver's earliest convenience."

As Jim turned the key, the '57 roared to life and the two of them sped off down the highway.

Meanwhile, Archie sat up, holding his head in his hands. "Oooh, my head," he moaned.

It was dark inside the trailer and as Archie's eyes adjusted to the small fragments of light coming in through the door, he remembered where he was.

"Oh, no...," he said. Then he realized the truck was moving.

"OH, NO!" he shouted.

He slowly made his way across the floor, holding onto the cases of beer as he side-stepped his way to the door. He tried to lift it, but it wouldn't budge.

"Jim's gonna kill me," he said to himself.

He sat down with his back against the trailer wall and held his head in his hands.

"Now what the heck am I gonna do?"

"Maybe I can get the driver's attention," he thought. He walked back across the wet floor to the opposite wall and pounded against it with his fists.

"Helloooo," he shouted! "Stop the truck! I'm in here!"

Inside the cab of the truck, Ben had the windows down and the volume cranked up on his radio, as he sang along with Willie Nelson to "Whiskey River." There was no way he could hear Archie pounding and yelling from inside the box trailer.

Archie gave up after a few minutes, as his hands, not to mention his busted finger, started to hurt as much as his head. He sat down again and started to think of how worried and upset Jim and Jimmy probably were right about now.

He'd just have to wait until the driver made his next stop. He prayed it wasn't all the way to Las Vegas.

Getting a bit thirsty, he took one of the beers from his tote bag. He then searched through his tote for his bottle opener. It wasn't there.

"Figures!" he shouted. "All this beer and no bottle opener. Talk about irony!"

He placed the beer back in the tote and looked one more time, but no bottle opener appeared. He couldn't even play checkers, because he had removed the checkers game along with his umbrella to make room for the beer.

Bored and upset, he took inventory of what he had. One SX-70 Land camera, one extra pack of film, one comb, a sweater, one ballpoint pen, one package of beef jerky and a pack of peppermint TicTacs.

He flipped open the TicTacs and popped two of the small mints in his mouth.

"Well, at least my breath is fresh," he thought to himself.

As he placed the TicTacs back in his tote, he stared at the Polaroid camera. Picking it up, he aimed it back at himself and pressed the button. The flash went off, partially blinding him. It took a minute or so for his eyes to readjust to the dark interior of the box trailer. He then peeled off the backing on the photo.

"Something for the scrapbook back home, he laughed."

There on the square picture, was poor Archie, or at least the top portion of his face. It was impossible to aim the camera well, so he had taken the picture with his best guess. He took a second shot, again blinding himself with the flash. This one turned out better. He got most of his head and torso in the shot. He took out the ballpoint pen and wrote on it: "My adventure inside a Schlitz box truck. June 1975."

He stared at the door as the truck sped along down the highway. Then, he suddenly got an idea. He worked his way back to the door and peered at the small sliver of light coming into the trailer. There was a narrow gap near the right side of the door toward the top. It was roughly six inches long and about a sixteenth of an inch wide.

"This just might work," he thought to himself.

He took another picture of himself with the Polaroid, this time making sure to get the boxes of beer in the background. He stared at his face, which almost looked pompous in the photo. He also had cut off the top of his head.

"Someone ought to invent a camera to take self-pictures someday," he muttered.

He snapped another picture, this time making sure to look helpless and frightened in the photo.

After five shots, the camera was empty. He replaced the film in the Polaroid and took another ten photos of himself. On each photo, he wrote a rescue message with the ballpoint pen.

He took the first picture and slid it sideways out of the gap and gave it a push. It worked! The photo was gone. Archie pressed his eye up to the gap and could see the picture float off to the right and land in the grass that grew along the shoulder. He didn't feel confident anyone would see that. He'd need to wait until he could see another vehicle pull up closer to the truck, then he would try again. He had fourteen more chances and then he'd be out of pictures.

About ten miles back, Jim and Jimmy were trying to catch up to the delivery truck.

"Are we speeding, Gramps?" asked Jimmy.

"Well, we're going a little over the limit, but I can't push this old girl too hard or she might overheat. We'll just stop at the first rest stop or station we see. I'm sure Archie's little joke is wearing off right about now and he'll want us to pick him up. I've got a good mind to drive right past him, should he turn up on the shoulder."

"At least we're both heading in the same direction," said Jimmy.

Jim looked over and smiled at his grandson. "Thanks for seeing the positive in the situation, pal."

Ben Jaworski wasn't sure how long the ice in his trailer would last in the ninety-two degree heat. He knew the next stop was a good forty miles ahead. The speedometer read 75 as he passed a small Volkswagen bus, driven by a couple of tie-dyed looking hippies. As the truck drove past them in the fast lane, a small paper square shot out from the back of the truck, followed quickly by another, then another.

"Litter-bug!" shouted the driver of the Volkswagen. The passenger flipped the bird to the truck as it sped away.

It was two miles later when ol' lead-foot Jaworski passed a trooper who had his black and white Plymouth Belvedere Pursuit, pulled off to the side of the road and hidden behind a billboard. The billboard read, "Keep America Clean, Don't Litter."

Ben was doing 79mph, when he sped past the trooper's patrol car. That's all it took as the trooper pulled out, shooting sand and dirt from the rear wheels. As the trooper gained on the truck. He could see small pieces of paper shooting out from the truck every so often. He was just about to put his lights and siren on, when one of the pieces slapped firmly and stuck to the driver's side windshield of the trooper's patrol car. There, was Archie's face with mouth open as if shouting something, staring right back at the trooper.

The trooper quickly pulled over to retrieve the picture from his windshield. He then read the message printed on it.
"PLEASE HELP! I'm trapped in a box truck going west on Route 40, headed toward Las Vegas!"

With lights on and siren wailing, the trooper quickly started off in pursuit of the truck and grabbed his CB radio transmitter.

"This is Car 22, I am in pursuit of a delivery truck on I-40 and have evidence of a possible kidnapping, about fifteen miles west of Ash Fork. Requesting back-up."

At first Ben couldn't hear anything with the radio blaring and him singing along with good ol' Willie. Then he saw the flashing lights. "Oh, crap!" he shouted. He immediately pulled off onto the shoulder and shut off the engine.

The trooper's patrol car pulled up right behind Ben, turning off the siren, but keeping the lights flashing. Stepping out of the patrol car, the trooper pointed his .357 Magnum revolver at the truck.

"Get out of the truck and keep your hands in the air."

Ben, scared as a draft horse in a barn fire, jumped out of the truck with hands held high.

"Put your hands on your head!" shouted the officer, who proceeded to cuff Ben and sit him down on the side of the road.

Just then, a second patrol car pulled up. That trooper got out and joined the first.

"Go ahead and open it," said the first trooper to the second, as he kept his weapon pointed at the truck door, not knowing what waited inside. The trooper opened the latch and pushed the door upwards.

"Hey guys, I'm so glad you found me, I was running out of pictures," said Archie as he sat on a case of Schlitz, holding his tote bag on his lap.

It took about fifteen minutes to get the whole thing straightened out, and fortunately, Ben only came away with a speeding ticket. Just as the troopers were about to take Archie away to the nearest patrol station, up pulled Jim and Jimmy in the convertible.

"Hey, my ride's here guys. I should be all set."

The trooper turned and looked at Jim.

"Do you know this guy?"

Jim smiled at the trooper. "I've never seen him before in my life," he said.

Chapter XIX

It took two days to cross Arizona, and the trio was now finally approaching the Grand Canyon. Following Jimmy's directions from the map, Jim turned onto Route 64 and followed the scenic lookout signs for Lipan Point.

Upon reaching the destination, Jim pulled over and the guys each climbed out of the Bel Air and approached the lookout. Silence overcame them at first, due to the sheer beauty of what was painted before them.

The colors of the canyon ranged from distant blue peaks to robust purples, and again from red to orange and then salmon. It was as if someone had access to every color and decided to make sure they were all used here in this one magical spot. Archie was the first to break the silence.

"I had no idea," he said, softly. "Only saw this in books."

"We studied this in geography class, Mr. Reynolds. If only my teacher could see this now," Jimmy responded.

Jim could say nothing. He had never traveled in his youth, outside of the military. Most of his life was spent in or near Philadelphia. He had no idea how breathtaking this would be.

His thoughts turned to Evelyn, as he wished they could have shared this together. They were always saving for their golden years. That's what she used to call it.

"She would have loved this," he thought.

But in a way, she was here with them now. Jim gazed over at Jimmy, as his grandson pointed out to the horizon, showing Archie the Colorado River in the distance, as it wound its way through the canyon, so many miles away.

Jim smiled and wiped his eyes. Like the canyon formation itself, where did all the time go?

The guys had a picnic lunch by the canyon, and Archie asked a passerby to take their picture with his Polaroid camera. As it slowly developed in the warm sun, they each hovered over the shot, exclaiming it was the best part of their vacation so far, and a time they would never forget.

The afternoon passed quickly, where the beauty of the canyon just seemed to go on forever, but it was time to find a place to stay. They all agreed they would come back again to this very spot before their trip was over.

As they climbed back into the car, Archie held up a travel brochure which featured Peach Springs, Arizona, and was angling for a stay-over in the nearby town.

"We gotta go to the Grand Canyon Caverns Inn," exclaimed Archie. "Just look at the pictures of this place!"

Archie held up the brochure so close to Jim's face, he almost couldn't see the road.

"In addition to the rooms and caverns, they also have a pool and a restaurant!"

"Okay, okay," said Jim. "You sold me. Don't need to twist my arm off."

When the guys arrived at the Grand Canyon Caverns Inn, it was unanimously decided to change into their suits and sit by the pool for a while. The sun was still high in the sky and the heat of late day made the small oasis all the more desirable.

In fact, just about everyone staying at the Inn seemed to have the same idea. There was hardly any place to sit, as all of the tables with sun umbrellas were taken, as was most of the pool seating as well.

Archie scanned the area and finally found two chaise lounges together close to the pool, but on the opposite side. Jimmy decided he didn't need a chair and just placed his towel on the ground beside Jim.

As they got settled in and Jim was plastering himself with sunscreen, Archie overheard the couple next to them ordering food, and any mention of the words menu, food or eating was not going to get past Archie's ears. He had the appetite of a sixteen-year-old.

He quickly flagged down the waitress and the guys each ordered a foot long hot dog with fries and a drink. As the waitress walked away, Archie took his Schlitz umbrella from his bag and threaded it through the straps on the back of his lounge chair, angling it precisely to block some of the sun's rays.

"For cryin' out loud, Arch," said Jim. "Why do you feel the need to constantly embarrass us?"

"Who's embarrassed?" asked Archie. "This is a collector's item, and a darn good sun shield."

"Suit yourself," said Jim, as he started to apply sunscreen to his chest and legs.

Archie and Jimmy jumped into the pool first, sending a splash of water out of the pool and onto Jim's legs. Looking to get even, Jim surprised them by taking off his glasses and jumping high in the air, cradling both legs. The cannonball hit the water with such a splash, it not only soaked Archie and Jimmy, but several people who were a good ten feet plus, away from the pool.

As Jim surfaced, he looked around and realized how far his splash had gone.

"Sorry," he said aloud. Then he looked at Jimmy and whispered, "Hey, if they don't want to get wet, they shouldn't sit so close to the pool."

Jimmy laughed and splashed Archie again before diving under to make his escape. When Jimmy surfaced, he found himself close to a group of kids who welcomed him and asked if he wanted to join them for a game of Marco Polo. Jimmy looked back at Gramps for approval, and Jim gave him the thumbs-up.

When their food arrived, Jim and Archie got out of the pool, while Jimmy stayed in for a while longer, as he was having too much fun playing Marco Polo.

"Man, you gotta love a good hot dog," said Archie, as he bit into his dog, which was topped with mustard and relish.

"Damn straight," said Jim as he took a huge bite of his chili dog.

"How about a game of checkers later?" asked Archie.

Jim didn't answer. He just looked straight ahead, as if frozen. Then he pounded on his chest with his fist and looked as if he was trying to cough.

Archie realized Jim was choking. He put down his own dog and got behind Jim and started to pound on his back with his fist, but Jim still looked to be choking as he struggled to cough and gasped for air.

"Look, that old man is choking!" one girl shouted to her parents.

Suddenly, a very large woman in her bathing suit and flip-flops, got up from her lounge chair and approached Jim with great haste. She announced she was a nurse from Wisconsin on vacation with her family, but Archie swore she could have been a defensive tackle for the Green Bay Packers.

"Step aside," she said, as she nudged Archie, who easily lost his balance and plopped back into his chair.

"I just learned this new procedure," she said, and proceeded to stand directly behind Jim and wrap her arms around his midsection. Then she began to pull upwards and inwards on his stomach area in short quick bursts.

At first, the only thing that happened was Jim's aviator sunglasses flew off his face and landed on the ground. Archie watched helplessly as Jim continued to gasp.

People were shocked at the scene, and some stood up from their chairs to see what was happening close to the pool. Then the nurse tried even harder and appeared to be almost lifting Jim off the ground. Archie was reminded of a special he saw on public television last month, of mating elephant seals in the Aleutian Islands.

With the next sharp thrust, Jim's false teeth shot out of his mouth and landed in the pool directly in front of him.

The kids who had stopped playing Marco Polo because of the commotion, instantly swam away from that corner of the pool, as if someone had dropped a piranha in it.

With the next inward thrust, Jim came off the ground again. His large arms flapped at his side. Suddenly, the stubborn, rubbery hunk of nitrates flew out of Jim's mouth like it was shot from a canon. The piece of hotdog bounced off the head of one of the kids near the pool, who shrieked upon its arrival, and landed in the gin and tonic of a woman who happened to be sleeping on her lounge chair and was unaware of the whole scene.

Jim was at last able to catch his breath. As he sat down, he thanked the nurse for her heroic effort.

"No problem," she said. "I'm glad I was here to help. And doubly glad to find out that the new Heimlich procedure they just started teaching, actually works!"

Jimmy reluctantly dove to the bottom and retrieved his grandfather's false teeth.

"Thanks," said Jim.

"Glad you're okay," said Jimmy.

"Wow, with all the beatings you took as a fighter, you almost got knocked out for good by a piece of hot dog," said Archie.

"That was scary," said Jim.

"You think? I thought she was going to break you in two," said Archie.

After they were done eating the guys decided a quiet tour of the caverns was in order.

The access to the caverns was by a large elevator that went over two hundred feet down. Their tour guide pointed out that the original discoverer of the caverns bought the property because he thought there was a vein of gold going through the rocks, only to find out later it was iron and rust he saw glimmering off the rocks. So, to make his investment pay off, he opened a tourist attraction. In the 1920's, customers would pay to be lowered down on a rope swing by a hand-cranked winch.

The whole contraption at the time was called "Dope on a rope."

"Hey, that's you," said Jim to Archie.

"Ha ha," replied Archie. "At last I wouldn't spit up hot dog all over the cave."

"Good one, Mr. Reynolds," said Jimmy, laughing.

As the group was walking around through the cool caverns, they could hear their voices echo off the cavern walls. The tour was forty minutes long and required a lot of walking up and down stairs through parts of the caverns. The cathedral area was gigantic and was at least as big as a football field underground. There was even a mummified bobcat from the mid-1800's.

Jimmy's highlight of the tour was when he was walking down a path and saw something shiny catch his eye. He walked off the path a few feet and thought it was a crystal perhaps. Upon picking it up, he discovered it sparkled brilliantly in the overhead lights.

"Look what I found, Gramps," said Jimmy, as he held it up to Jim.

"Finders, keepers," said Archie.

"Now wait a minute, Arch. We have to see what Jimmy found first."

Jimmy looked a bit confused as he showed it to his grandfather, for it did not match any of the crystals listed on the explorer's tour sheet they were given.

"Do you know what it is?" asked Jimmy. "Is it a rare crystal?"

"It looks to me like a diamond, but it's definitely a cut gem," said Jim.

"What does that mean?" asked Jimmy.

"It means that the stone has been cut and polished, and someone most likely lost it while on the tour. It could have come loose from its setting."

"Do I get to keep it?"

"Well, just take a minute and think if it was something you lost. How would you feel?"

"I guess we should see if they have a lost and found," said Jimmy. "That's what we have at school if someone leaves something on the playground.

"I knew you'd think of something smart like that," said Jim. "Why don't you hold on to it for now and we'll see after the tour if we can locate the right person to speak to."

When the tour was complete, the guys stopped in the gift shop, where a woman was behind the counter.

Jimmy walked up and placed the diamond on the counter and told the woman he had found it down in the caverns.

"Oh, my goodness, thank you," said the woman. "Someone came in yesterday and claimed they had lost the diamond from their engagement ring. Let me see if they are still staying here."

The woman looked through some paperwork and confirmed they were still here.

"Yes, they are still here. Her and her fiancé, are here on vacation from New York. She's going to be thrilled when she finds out you found her diamond," said the woman.

She shook Jimmy's hand and asked him to wait a minute. She walked into a back room and came out a few minutes later with a gift certificate, which she handed to Jimmy.

"A good deed deserves a reward," she said.

Jimmy looked at the certificate which was made out to the sum of twenty dollars.

"Wow, thank you!" he shouted. "This is more than I make on my paper route in a whole week."

"You're most welcome. You can use it on anything in the restaurant or this store," the woman said.

That evening, after a late dinner, Jimmy asked if he could have a few minutes to browse through the store. As he looked over the merchandise, he found postcards, books and maps, small rocks which were from the caverns, and T-shirts which bore the name and logo of the caverns.

But it was a small display case which caught his attention.

It was filled with necklaces, which were made from crystals that had been found in the caverns and polished to a beautiful finish.

The piece that caught Jimmy's eye was a necklace made up of a dozen small crystals that were strung on a silver chain. The small stones gleamed like pearls as they caught the light.

He looked around the store some more, but came back to the same necklace. He wanted to buy it as a gift for his mom. Even though he hadn't met her yet, he felt compelled to get it. He could imagine her smile when she received the necklace.

He looked at the tag and it read twenty-two dollars.

Digging into his back pocket for his wallet, he looked inside to find a few dollars and some loose change from his paper route. Together with the certificate, he confirmed he had enough.

The woman commended Jimmy on his choice, and took the necklace from the case and placed in in a pink box with a soft piece of cotton batting to protect it. She then wrapped the neat package with a pink bow.

As Jimmy walked out of the gift shop, he was beaming with pride. He couldn't wait to surprise his mom with the necklace.

The next day, the trio drove away from Peach Springs and headed southwest on Route 66. It was later that afternoon when they were getting close to the town of Kingman. Jimmy checked the road map again to see how far away they were.

"About twenty minutes more and we should be there," said Jimmy.

"Hey, Arch, what's the address again that the studio gave us?"

Archie took out his note pad and flipped back through the pages.

"Looks like 3622 Skylark Road."

Jimmy helped Jim get to the right street, by talking through the directions on the map they had picked up at a local gas station. Jim navigated through the maze of blocks, each containing roughly twenty-four houses situated quite close to each other.

"With all this open space, you'd think they'd put these things a little farther apart," said Archie.

Jim crept along slowly until he came up to number 3622. The small, single-floor house was on a corner, and there was a small tree in the tiny front yard. What little grass there was, looked to be mostly burnt from the sun. Jim pulled up to the curb and parked.

The house itself looked like a type of stucco and was painted a salmon-pink coral color. There was one car in the driveway, a green Dodge Coronet, and the right front quarter panel was primer gray.

"Is this where my mom lives?" asked Jimmy.

"It's the address that the studio gave us, " answered Jim, double checking the number on the mail box.

Jim looked over at Archie and then Jimmy. Look guys, I'm gonna walk up to the door solo and see if this is the right place. I think it's best if you wait for me here."

"Okay," said Jimmy, as he pulled out his pink gift box and straightened the bow, which had gotten a bit flattened in the bag. He then remembered the album cover he had brought with them.

"Here, take the record, Gramps."

Jim took the Sherri Summer album from Jimmy, and walked up to the front door and rang the doorbell. Right away a dog started barking. It sounded like a small dog to Jim, either a Pomeranian or a Chihuahua.

Jim could hear footsteps approaching from inside and the front door opened. A small Hispanic woman stared back at him through the screen door.

"Can I help you?" she asked in broken English.

"Yes, My name is Jim Dillon and I'm looking for Terri Dillon. I was told she might be here. She might also be using her maiden name, which is Summer."

Jim held up the album cover to show the woman Terri's picture which was on the front.

"Yes," said the woman. "I think she rented the house before I did. She had left me a forwarding address for her mail, but that was several years ago. Give me just a minute, please."

The woman walked away, with the small barking dog following her.

"Quiet, Linda," she shouted at the Pomeranian.

A few minutes later, she walked back to the screen door and opened the latch. She handed Jim a small piece of note paper.

"Her mail stopped coming a long time ago, but I still kept this in the back of my kitchen drawer, just in case," she said.

Jim looked at the paper. It read: Terri Summer, 220 MacFarland Avenue, Indian Springs, Nevada.

"Thank you ma'am," said Jim. "Would you know how far that would be from here?"

"It's about two and a half hours from here," she said. "It's a small town, north of Las Vegas."

"Much appreciated," said Jim, as he tipped his hat, smiled and walked back to the car.

"Well, we have another address to find," said Jim to Archie and Jimmy.

"You mean she doesn't live here?" asked Jimmy, sounding dejected, as he placed his pink gift-wrapped box back in its bag.

"Not anymore pal," said Jim. "But I got a solid lead to where she forwarded her mail, so we'll just follow the trail, okay?"

Jim gave Archie the note so he could copy the address onto his pad as well. Jimmy straightened up in his seat, looked on the road map and found Indian Springs, north of Las Vegas, just as the woman had said.

"Here it is Gramps. Indian Springs," said Jimmy as he pointed out the town on the map to Jim.

Jim looked up at the afternoon sun. "Let's head back to the Inn and get a good meal in our bellies and a good night's sleep," said Jim. "Then we can decide how to follow up on this new lead."

Chapter XX

Jim allowed the desert dust to settle before stepping out of his car. He looked up at the "Cup-o-Joe" diner sign for a few moments and then at the trailer, which looked to be attached to the back of the diner.

"Kind of a strange place for a home address," he thought to himself.

There were a few trucks in the parking lot. The kind that drove around with dings and dents in their fenders from a history of swiping a few guard rails. At least they proved the place was actually open and not just another wild goose chase.

He peered into the back of one of the trucks as he walked past, which held several empty beer cans; no doubt they were the cause of the majority of the dings and dents. He was confident he made the correct decision to leave Archie and Jimmy at the Grand Canyon Caverns Inn. They were enjoying the pool so much, and just in case this was a dead end, it would be easier on Jimmy this way.

He stepped inside and took off his cap.

"Sit anywhere you'd like," said the tall, blonde waitress from behind the counter. "Terri will be with you in a minute."

The hair slightly lifted on the back of his neck, at the mention of her name. Was this really the right spot after all?

It was a small joint. An oasis in the desert, with a twelve-seat counter and just as many small booths. A short, Mexican-looking guy manned the grill. He placed a plate on the window ledge and rang a bell.

"Orda' up," he shouted in a Mexican accent.

Four other customers were seated at the counter. Jim walked past them and sat in one of the booths toward the rear of the diner. He looked back to where the restrooms might be and noticed a small hallway which led further back, probably to the connected trailer he had seen from outside.

At the edge of the table toward the wall was one of those coin operated mini juke boxes. There was a piece of tape across the coin slot that read "broken."

Then he heard a shuffle of feet from the hallway behind him. Out came a young brunette, with the classic pencil tucked into the barrette which held her hair up. She walked past Jim, grabbed a menu, napkin and silverware and walked back to his booth.

Jim stared up at the face he knew so well. She had aged sightly. Not the same as the picture from her record album jacket, and clearly much different from her days in Philly, but rather a more mature kind of pretty.

"Coffee?" she asked.

"Yes," replied Jim. "Just black."

"Special today is biscuits and sausage gravy. Would you like a few minutes?"

"Uh... yes," Jim answered, as he took the menu from her hand.

All these miles and his mind had gone blank. He thought it would have been easier, hoping she would have called out his name, but she didn't seem to recognize him. He knew he had changed, too. Not that 64 was old, but the loss of his wife and then his son, had obviously taken its toll, sculpting an older, weathered face and grayer hair.

He was second guessing himself on not bringing Jimmy. But he knew it was a long shot as to whether she'd come back. He couldn't stand to see his grandson's heart break if she decided to say no, right there in front of him. Better to do it this way.

Too many questions flooded his mind. Had this life made her callous and cold? Was she anything remotely like what he remembered back when she and Danny were dating?

She walked back a minute later with a mug of hot coffee and gently placed it down in front of him.

"What'll you have?" she asked.

"I'll have two eggs over easy with some home fries and rye toast please," answered Jim, slowly.

She began to turn away when he called out her name.

"Terri..."

She spun around and looked at him closely, waiting for him to continue, but not quite sure how he knew her name. She wore no name badge.

"Terri, It's me, Jim... Jim Dillon."

Terri's eyes grew slightly wider. She looked shocked, but not scared, to Jim's relief.

"Oh, my God," she whispered.

She promptly sat down in the booth directly across from him and stared at his face, remembering the features she knew and putting together the puzzle that time had created.

"Why... why are you here?

"I needed to find you... I mean, we needed to find you.

"We? You mean you and Danny?

"No. Terri, I know this may be hard to hear, but Danny's been gone a while now. He died of cancer in '69. We tried to find you, but had no idea where you had gone."

"Oh my God, I'm so sorry."

Suddenly, Terri's eyes started to well up, and Jim reached across the table and took her hand in his.

"Terri, Danny never took Jimmy to the agency. He decided to keep him. He raised a fine young boy, and now Jimmy lives with me."

"He named him after you... I'm glad. You and Danny were always very close."

"He's a great kid, Terri. A really great kid. I look at him every day across from me at the breakfast table and I see Danny in his face... but I also see you."

"I'm sorry Jim. I made so many mistakes... so many mistakes. I don't deserve a son; and besides, he probably hates me for leaving like I did."

"No, he doesn't, Terri. He wants to meet you. He's staying with a good friend of mine back at an Inn, not too far off the main highway."

Jim reached into his shirt pocket and pulled out a Polaroid photo Archie had taken of Jimmy and him. He placed the photo in Terri's hand.

"We came all the way out here for you, Terri. It doesn't matter what you did in the past. Our mistakes make us stronger."

Terri blotted her eyes with her apron, and placed her hand over her mouth, trying not to cry out as she stared at the picture of her son.

"He's beautiful," she whispered. "How on earth did you find me?"

"It's a long story that started when Jimmy and a friend brought home one of your record albums. We drove out to where the record company told us you might be, but found a woman living there who gave us your forwarding address."

"Great place, right? I know it's not much, but I get a roof over my head and free meals here."

"I understand. Everyone has to take what they can get at some point in their life. Look, I'm not going to be here on this earth forever, Terri. My grandson deserves a chance to be with his mom. Won't you at least meet him?"

"I... I don't know. I mean, then what? I'm tied to this place Jim. It's not like back home in Philly. It's different out here."

"Look, I still have the place on Oak Street. You can come back and move in with us. We can be a family again."

"No, you don't understand Jim. I can't leave here. I owe Rick money. A lot of money. He owns this place. I work here to pay off my debt to him. I sleep in the back, and that's my life for now."

"What kind of a life is that?"

"It's all I have right now, Jim. I can't leave, and I don't want to drag Jimmy into this type of life. It wouldn't be right."

"How much do you owe this guy?"

"A lot, Jim."

"How much, Terri?"

"I've been working it off, but I still owe over fourteen thousand dollars. He covered my first record deal... and... my gambling debts. Look, I told you I made some big mistakes."

Jim didn't have an answer for that one. He just sighed and patted Terri's hand with his.

"Terri, we're family, and family sticks together. We'll find a way to pay this guy and get you in the clear. I have a little money saved from my fighting days, and maybe that combined with my military pension, we can pay this guy off over time."

"You don't fully understand, Jim. I cannot leave here until I pay him. Rick's got connections. He'd have me followed as soon as I tried to leave, and then what? It's just no good. It's like he owns me.

"Nobody owns anybody, Terri. Not even someone with connections."

"Like I said, you don't understand, Jim."

"Okay, just give me some time to think on that for now. Leaving here or not, Jimmy's your son. Can he at least meet you? We drove over two thousand miles, Terri."

"I don't know. I'm off my shift at seven tonight, but I don't own a car. What were you thinking?"

"I'll swing by and pick you up here at quarter to eight. The four of us can all go out to dinner some place nice. My treat, okay?"

"I guess so. But this seems so fast. I'm scared, Jim. What'll I say to Jimmy?"

"If I know Jimmy, he'll break the ice for you. The rest will come naturally. You're still young, Terri. You have the rest of your life sitting there, right in front of you - and the chance to be there for Jimmy. You may have missed some great moments, but the best may be yet to come. Don't you think it's time to take that first step?"

Terri nodded and blotted her eyes again and got up from the booth. She walked over to the counter and placed Jim's order. Looking back, she smiled at Jim. It was something she hadn't done for quite a while... and it felt good.

Chapter XXI

Jimmy was nervous as he walked up to the trailer door. Jim had prompted him to do so, explaining that as a young man, going to the door was a gentleman's thing to do.

Jim and Archie stayed in the Chevy, watching as Jimmy knocked on the glass window.

"One minute, I'll be right there," could be heard from outside.

Along with his pink gift box, Jimmy held a small bouquet of flowers that he had bought from a gas station on the strip. They were his idea, and Jim was proud of him for having not just the idea, but the courage to go through with this.

The door to the trailer opened and Terri looked beautiful as she stepped out into the evening light. She wore a light blue sun dress and her hair was down around her shoulders. She looked so different from when Jim had seen her last.

"Wow," said Archie. "She's gorgeous! "

Jimmy handed her the flowers with arms extended. Terri took them from him and just stopped for a moment, taking in the look of her son's face. Trying to see what Jim had described to her earlier in the day. She could see Danny. But she also could see more. It was just a moment's glance, but it was confirmed. She saw some of herself.

"Thank you so much. These are beautiful, Jimmy," she said. "I'm going to put these in water if you don't mind and I'll be right out."

She wanted to invite them in, but she was embarrassed by the place. The trailer was small and her room was just one section of it. The other portion contained Rick's office. Terri wanted to set a good first impression, and a tour of the small trailer wasn't on the itinerary.

A minute later, Terri closed the door behind her and Jimmy reached up for her hand, which she gladly took. He then presented her with the small pink box.

"This for you, too," he said with a slight shyness in his voice.

"Why, thank you," she replied. "I had no idea you were going to bring gifts."

"Go ahead and open it," said Jimmy, eagerly awaiting her expression.

As Terri slid off the pink ribbon and opened the box, she gasped, overtaken by the beautiful gesture of the gift.

"It's a beautiful necklace," she said. "I'm going to put it on right now for this special occasion."

As Terri put on the necklace, she asked Jimmy how it looked.

"Fantastic," he replied, smiling.

As Terri and Jimmy walked up to the car, Archie introduced himself and opened the door so Terri could sit in back with Jimmy.

It was a warm evening and the top was down on the Chevy. The sun was soon to go down and there was a faint promise of stars above as they drove off to dinner.

Terri looked over at Jimmy again, but found herself frozen, as if her mind had just gone blank. So many thoughts flooded her head on how this boy was really her son.

"We found your record album back in Philly," said Jimmy. "My pal Sam and I really liked the song "A Place In My Heart." That's when Gramps recognized you on the cover. We decided that my summer vacation was the best time to come find you. You certainly traveled far to come make records."

"I did at that," said Terri.

She searched for more conversation, feeling a little self-conscious.

"Your friend Sam... does he go to your school?"

"Oh, Sam's not a he, she's a she," said Jimmy. Her family is a customer on my paper route. That's how we met. Her mom makes great chocolate chip cookies. She puts raisins in them, and they're my favorite."

"That's funny, I've always liked them with raisins, too. How long have you had your paper route?"

"For only a couple months, but Gramps showed me how to throw a good paper, and with my other job at Mr. Reynolds' antique store, I bought a new bike, so now I can do my route in half the time."

"He's a good helper and he's got an eye for good stuff," said Archie, chiming in.

The ride to the restaurant took roughly twenty minutes, and during that time, Jimmy held up the majority of the conversation, putting Terri more and more at ease. He described the crazy characters in his fourth grade class, their crabby teacher, his paper route customers, and spent extra time explaining his baseball card collection in detail.

By the time they arrived at the restaurant, Terri had knowledge of most of the Phillies' batting averages. Even though baseball wasn't quite her thing, she found herself fascinated by his passion for details and how much Jimmy loved the sport. She began thinking of what she might have missed over all these years.

"Well, here we are folks," said Jim. "Laurie's Steak House and Lounge. Supposed to have the best rib-eye this side of Kansas City."

As they stepped inside, the host seated them next to a fountain, which was a small replica of a waterfall. It was all quite fancy and Jimmy looked proud. Terri was thrilled when Jimmy pulled out the chair for her to sit down; yet another tip from Gramps.

The waiter came over to their table and took drink orders.

"I heard music," said Archie to the waiter.

"They have dancing in that room after nine. You should check it out, it's quite fun, and they installed a disco ball last week."

"Maybe we will," said Archie.

Jim ordered a bottle of wine to share with Terri. Jimmy asked for a Coke and Archie, his usual Schlitz.

"Thank you for asking me to dinner," said Terri. "This is really nice. I don't get to go out to much anymore."

"Why not?" asked Jimmy.

"Well, I usually have to get up early to open the diner every morning, and on my salary, it's not something I can afford often. But it's much appreciated. I loved the flowers Jimmy, and especially the beautiful necklace. Thank you, again."

"You bet," said Jimmy. "They reminded me of the flowers on the cover of your album. Did you make many records out here?"

"Uh, not exactly. In fact, just the one. But at one point I was working on a few new songs."

"Well, like I said, we thought your album had good songs. Sam and I both liked it."

"Thank you, Jimmy. Next time, I'll bring my guitar and play you a few verses of what I've been working on."

"Do you think you might be coming home with us to Philly?"

Terri feared that question was going to eventually come up. She looked into his face and wanted so much to give him the answer he hoped for, but couldn't lie.

A few seconds passed and then Jim jumped in to break the awkward silence.

"Well, pal, Terri has some responsibilities here that she has to meet, so we're just going to give her some time to clear those up. We can discuss her coming home at another time. But, hey, look at this menu. These look like some great steaks!"

Terri looked over at Jimmy as he ordered his meal from the waiter. Dressed in his best blue button-down shirt and khaki slacks, he looked like a little man. He ordered a cheeseburger over the steak, but did it in such an adult manner, Terri almost started crying.

She thought about how much time she had wasted. From the time Jimmy first started taking steps, until this very moment – it was lost. It hung in limbo somewhere between her dreams and reality. He had grown up into the young man she sat next to at this very table, only he had done it without her. He had memories from all those years, but none with her.

It was going to be difficult to start from this point. But she felt a determination now, like she never had before.

Where was the determination back then? Why were those years filled with such selfishness and self-pity?

She almost envied Danny for the time he had with Jimmy. But Danny was gone now and this was her time to make things right, and by God she was going to succeed.

The evening was filled with stories of laughter and wonder. Jimmy told Terri about dancing with Dad, his passion for music, his field trip to the zoo, the time Jim had made his Halloween costume out of a box and he trick-or-treated as a pack of Camel cigarettes.

Too many stories to tell in one evening, but Terri looked forward to hearing them all, and she told him so.

After dinner, they walked over to the dance room and sat at a table, where they ordered some dessert. Jimmy got himself a hot fudge sundae. Jim took a pass, but Archie ordered a slice of apple pie, with Terri following suit.

The music suddenly got Archie's attention as the DJ started to play KC and The Sunshine Band's "Get Down Tonight."

"Hey, I had just got this on vinyl a few weeks back," said Archie. "Great album."

"You like disco?" asked Jim.

"Sure, back home, the girls down at the Polish club dance more to this stuff, than they do polkas."

Terri looked at Jimmy across the table, who had just finished his ice cream sundae. "Would you like to dance?"

"Uh, I really don't know how; but maybe you can show me."

Terri took Jimmy's hand and was all smiles as they both walked out on the dance floor. There was no other guy she would rather be dancing with. Terri showed him how to loosen up and to move with the rhythm.

"Come on Jim, let's join them. You must still have plenty of moves from your time in the ring. Come on!"

"Thanks for the recommendation, pal. But this really isn't my speed."

"Well, I guess that leaves me," said Archie, with a big smile on his face.

When Archie's white loafers hit the dance floor, he almost looked like he knew what he was doing, with moves that were a combination of disco and swing dancing, which he knew from his younger years.

But halfway through the song, he started to look like he was trying too hard. Jim laughed to himself as the harder Archie tried, the more ridiculous he looked.

His arms were flapping at his side as he lifted his knees in what looked to be a cross between a Russian cossack dance and a chicken imitation.

Archie was just one of those people that you could never call graceful. It reminded Jim of the time when they were much younger and using Archie's metal detector in an abandoned lot to look for old coins. Archie had come across a rat snake that day, which had thrown him into such a panic, he had run off that lot like he was shot out of a canon, arms waving in the air and knees flying high.

Jim slapped his thigh, he was laughing so hard. Tears formed at the corner of his eyes from the memory.

Now Archie began stomping his white loafers back and forth and started doing a lot of upward pointing, extending his arm and sticking out his index finger skyward, like he was trying to get someone to look up at a passing plane.

"It's gotta be something he saw on television," said Jim, to himself.

As a waiter walked along the edge of the dance floor to deliver a tray of drinks to a nearby table, one of Archie's repetitive finger jabs, caught the waiter in the eye.

The waiter immediately lost his balance, along with tray, as he went stumbling backwards. Drinks went flying and landed at the table of a party of two men along with their dates. The women each shrieked upon being soaked.

Their dates, who looked to be in their forties, immediately stood up and were clearly upset.

"Look what you did, you clumsy idiot," shouted one of the men who advanced toward Archie.

Terri, feeling she knew what was about to happen next, gently led Jimmy off the dance floor and back to their table.

One of the guys swung at Archie, hitting him on the side of the face and knocking him backwards.

"Oh, just great," said Jim as he stood up. "Wait here," he said to Terri and Jimmy. "I'll be right back."

Jim crossed the dance floor in a hurry, to where Archie was sprawled out on the floor and helped him up.

"Why don't you pick on someone your own size?" Jim said to the guy, who still looked steamed.

"Butt out, pops," said the guy, as he came at Archie again with his fist cocked back.

Jim quickly stepped in front of Archie, who was clearly still dazed and batted away the man's forearm.

"Butt this!" said Jim, as he threw a hard left jab at the guy, which sent him stumbling backwards onto the lap of his girlfriend, who shrieked as the two fell backwards onto the floor.

The guy's friend stepped in, and swung at Jim. He was big, but slow. Jim's old reflexes kicked in as he side-stepped, blocking the punch with his own forearm and threw a jab in return, then rolled his hips and followed up with a quick uppercut, which sent the man backwards, and onto the table.

Just then, three large bouncers stepped into the fray and broke up the whole thing.

It was an hour later, when Jim, Archie and Jimmy dropped Terri back at her trailer at the diner. The place was still open and Terri asked them to come in for a cup of coffee. "Sure," said Jim. "I think I could use one."

"Sorry for the trouble tonight," said Archie, as he sipped his cup of coffee across from Terri in the booth.

"It's okay, Archie," said Terri. "I know one of the bouncers, who eats breakfast here on Sundays. Nothing was broken, except for a few glasses."

"That was wild," exclaimed Jimmy. "Especially when Gramps socked that guy in the face."

"I shouldn't have done that, Jimmy. Temper got the best of me. Just glad no one was hurt bad. I think the waiter got the worst of it. His eye looked pretty swollen shut from Archie's left 'poke'."

"I'll stick to waltzes and polkas from now on," said Archie.

The group was interrupted when Terri's boss, Rick, walked over to the table.

"Friends of yours, Terri?"

"Yes. Guys, this is my boss, Rick. Rick this is Jim, his grandson Jimmy and Archie."

Terri didn't want to mention anything about her son to Rick. Not that she was ashamed, but rather felt it was none of his business.

"Nice to meet ya," said Rick.

"Don't forget you're open tomorrow morning, Terri," said Rick, as he walked away.

"What a sweetheart," said Jim.

"Yep, that's Rick," said Terri.

"Who's a sweetheart?" asked Jimmy.

"Just a figure of speech," said Jim. "Finish your cocoa, and we'll hit the road. Terri's got to get up early tomorrow."

After they had said goodnight to Terri for the evening, they drove back down the strip. Every glowing sign seemed to shout to them. It was as if the whole city was on holiday.

"What an electric bill they must have," Archie blurted out.

"You said it," said Jim. "Dinner was good, Jimmy?"

"Yeah, Gramps, real good."

Jimmy's head was filled with questions. He couldn't understand why Terri had to stay there and keep working and couldn't come back home with them. Jim had told Archie everything Terri told him, but when it came to Jimmy, he sugar-coated the reason. Telling Jimmy that Terri simply had to pay some bills before she could come back home, was the easiest thing he could think of. Explaining to his grandson how his mom essentially owed money to the mob was not on the agenda.

As they drove slowly along looking at the signs, Archie suddenly blurted out again, "Jim, pull over here for a minute".

Jim pulled to the curb and quickly put the car in park, thinking Archie was about to be sick or something. "Haven't you had enough excitement for the evening, Arch?"

"Look at that sign, it says DRAUGHTS."

"Arch, I think you had enough beer with dinner. Whatta ya' say we head back to the Inn and hit the hay for the evening."

"No, not beer," said Archie. "It says right there: Draughts Tournament."

"Well, what the heck is that?" asked Jim. "We both know you can't drink anyone under the table."

"...or dance," said Jimmy snickering from the back seat.

"It's checkers, Jim!" shouted Archie. "Draughts is the professional term for checkers."

Archie jumped out of the convertible so fast, he forgot to shut the car door. His white loafers scampered up the steps to the entrance of the hall. Jim and Jimmy locked eyes and smiled, wondering what Archie's latest brainstorm might lead to. Five minutes later, Archie returned to the car with an excited look on his face.

"Jim, I just figured out how we're going to help Terri get out of her jam. There's a checkers tournament two days from now and I'm going to enter it. The grand prize is fifteen thousand dollars!"

"That's your great idea? Look Arch, number one, you're not a professional player. Number two, don't these tournament things have entry fees… big entry fees?"

"Sure, but I kick your butt all the time in checkers. In fact, did you know that I was the high school checkers champ of Poughkeepsie, New York before our family moved to the city?"

"Gee, Arch, that's fantastic. What are the odds the guys in this tournament are all from Poughkeepsie? Okay, maybe you're better than I think you are, but what about the entrance fee?"

"It's only five hundred," shot back Archie.

"What?!" shouted Jim. "Five hundred! Where are you going to find that kind of money in two days? We're living with just enough to get by while we're out here, and I'm not touching any of Jimmy's college money I got tucked away. It took me a long time just to put aside a few grand."

"It's easy. There are pawn stores everywhere. We'll pawn your Bel Air."

"Pawn my baby? Noooo way, Arch. Bad idea!"

"Jim, I have a feeling I can win. It's like it was meant to be. We'll pawn it and then when I win, we'll buy it back."

"No way. Too risky. There's got to be another way."

"Jim, what other way? This was meant to be. I can win this thing!"

Jim looked at the passion and confidence in Archie's face. He then thought about the odds of stumbling upon a checkers tournament, and he thought about all the times Archie gave him a shellacking on the town green. He thought of Jimmy, too, and how badly he wanted to see them live together, happy and with a fresh start.

"Well, Arch, I guess if we're gonna take a gamble, this is the town to do it in. Let's get you signed up, pal!"

Chapter XXII

Archie left the motel with his checkerboard, camera and a can of Schlitz, and spent all of the next day at the Clark County Library, studying every book he could get his hands on for checkers tournament play. The more he read, the more excited he got about the tournament.

Archie had always been a natural when it came to checkers. It was his relaxed and risky demeanor that often was his ally. Plus, he always got a real kick out of baiting his opponent into a move.

That's where checkers had a different style of play than chess. With chess, moves are voluntary, but with some tournament play versions of checkers, if an opponent baited you to an open jump, you had to make that jump. You simply could not play or move a different piece. You had to play the piece that was presented with the open jump or jumps.

That same afternoon, Terri had finished her shift and asked Jim if would be okay to spend time with Jimmy at the canyon. Jim thought it was a great idea and even offered to stay behind so Jimmy could have some quality time with his mom. Jim was nervous at first about Jimmy going off alone with Terri, but Jim knew if this was going to work, he needed to trust Terri and this felt like a good place to start.

Terri picked up Jimmy in a small Volkswagen convertible. The front right fender was primer gray, but the rest of the car was a faded red. In the back seat was her guitar case and next to that was a backpack.

"I thought we'd spend the afternoon at the canyon," she said to Jimmy. "I know a real nice spot where we can picnic, and I brought some sandwiches for lunch. If you're interested, I know a spot near the south rim where we can rent a couple of horses for a trail ride."

Jimmy was thrilled with the idea. Jim agreed it would be okay and Terri promised to have him back around sunset.

"You brought your guitar," said Jimmy. "I was hoping I could hear you play a little."

"...and I was hoping you'd like to hear some of my music," said Terri.

As Terri pulled up to her favorite spot near the south rim of the canyon, she asked Jimmy to help by carrying her guitar for her. They hiked only a few hundred feet to a scenic spot that was shaded by two ancient cedar trees. Terri told Jimmy that this was one of her favorite places to come sit, relax and play her guitar.

"It's so beautiful here," said Jimmy. "I can see why you like it here so much."

"It is truly like no other place I've been," said Terri.

Terri spread out a large blanket with colorful southwestern patterns and then unpacked their sandwiches and water.

"Is this the reason you came out here?" asked Jimmy.

At first Terri hesitated. It was a big question that deserved more than a quick answer. The deeper question was, "why did she leave the family?" There was so much she wanted to share with Jimmy, but not all of her past was something that she felt comfortable sharing. Yet, if they were going to have a relationship of mother and son, it would need to be based on honesty. She thought about the best way to share some of her past with her son.

"Maybe I can tell you a little about my youth and that might help answer your question."

Jimmy nodded as he bit into the ham and cheese sandwich.

"I grew up on a small farm in Elk County, Pennsylvania. It's still there today. My brother Michael helps my dad run it. When I was in high school, I learned to play the guitar. My mom had bought it for me for my birthday one summer, and I got pretty good at it. Self taught, I guess you could say.

Well, my parents had gotten divorced that same year, and my mom ended up leaving the farm the following spring. I'm not sure why. I was a little younger than you are now. I guess they just couldn't fix their differences. But I knew they both loved me.

All through middle school and high school I took that guitar just about everywhere I roamed on the farm. I started to get really good at playing and started to write some of my own music. After I graduated from high school, I moved to Philadelphia. I just wanted to be where it was busier, and while the farm always felt like home, there just wasn't enough to keep me there. I felt I needed a new start and I wanted to explore what else was out there.

I had written several songs by that time and that's when I started working part-time in different pubs, playing songs for customers. A lot of people seemed to like my music. That's when I met Danny, your dad."

"Were you and my dad the same age?" asked Jimmy.

"Danny was a few years older than me. He had grown up in Philadelphia and was going to college for business. He would often come hear me play during the evening when he didn't have classes.

"We dated for a few years. After he graduated from college he wanted to open a local business in Philadelphia, and I wanted to pursue my singing career. I fell into a group of friends who said a lot of musicians were heading to the west coast to try and pursue their music out in California. Your dad wanted to stay in Philly and I wanted to see what else was out there. It was also around that time, I became pregnant."

Terri hesitated and took a sip of her water. She smiled lovingly at Jimmy.

"Go on mom, what happened next?" asked Jimmy.

"After you were born, I... I got scared."

"Scared of what?" asked Jimmy.

"Scared of not being a good enough mom, I guess. Scared of that kind of responsibility. Maybe scared of not fulfilling my music dreams. I felt you deserved better than I could give you. I know now that was a mistake, I just didn't know it at the time."

"And that's when you moved away?"

"Yes, Jimmy. That's when I moved away. At first, I moved to Colorado with a few friends for about a year. We played in Steamboat Springs and continued to write songs. That's where I heard about a small studio in Las Vegas that was accepting new artists. So once again, I moved west and settled in Las Vegas. I thought about you often, and I'd imagine you were in a much better place than with a mom who had a need to keep moving.

"I ended up signing a record contract and sold my first songs to the record company. I agreed to receive a small amount of royalties for any records they sold. That first album did okay in the beginning, but it didn't produce the millions of sales I had dreamed about. The contract said I was to produce another album within two years or I'd be liable for partial payment on what I was forwarded. I know it sounds complicated, but contracts can be like that. That second record just never happened. Somehow, I just couldn't get inspired to write like I had before. It was like I was surrounded by all this beauty, but couldn't find the inspiration to put down the words. It's hard to explain, but I think it has something to do with sharing your life with someone. It seems like everything I had written had something to do with my life experiences up to that point."

"I think I understand," said Jimmy. "Before I met my friend Sam, the neighborhood felt kind of lonely. Now after school, she helps me with my papers and we ride bikes together, and it just feels better."

"Yes, it feels something like that. I know I probably feel more like a stranger right now than your mom, but I'm hoping we can change all that."

"Me too," said Jimmy. "You sure make a good sandwich," he said, as he polished off the remainder of his ham and cheese.

As they both looked out onto the canyon, Terri opened her guitar case and started to play some opening chords to a song she had just started working on. Jimmy loved the way she played. It was a gentle flowing rhythm that reminded him of when the rain would fall in the evenings back home, and the way the trees would make noise outside his window when the wind blew. He watched as her fingers worked the strings, and then she started to sing:

"The spirit wind blew through the night,
and gently spoke to me,
It spoke of one traveling through the plains,
and love would be the key.

He looked at me and spoke my name,
with eyes that were so bright,

and now I know my spirit can take flight."

Jimmy smiled and applauded. "That's good," he said.

"I wrote it just last night," said Terri. "After we had met for the first time. Maybe, you were the inspiration I was looking for."

Terri and Jimmy enjoyed the sun, which seemed to change the colors of the canyon as it moved lower in the sky. It was their first picnic together and each of them was hoping that many more would follow.

Chapter XXIII

The next day, Archie went back to the library and continued reading books on the various styles of play until he could absorb no more. He felt he was as ready as he could be, and was eager to face off against some of the best players the game had to offer.

When the day of the tournament arrived, Archie was a little nervous, but also excited at the same time. Jim had called a cab and the guys picked up Terri at her trailer so they all could head out for a bite to eat before the tournament started.

Jim saw the nervousness in Archie's face. He had known his pal for so many years, and seeing this side of him was rare. He did his best to try and settle him down.

"You know, before a fight, every fighter has his way of loosening up. Some guys don't like to eat, while others do. Me, I'd eat a half dozen eggs and drink a quart of milk about two hours before the fight," he said. "I always thought it gave me the energy to do my best."

"I like that thinking," said Archie. "I think I'll get a cheeseburger with bacon and cheddar; and maybe a side of fries, too."

After dinner, the four took a cab over to the "Red Carpet" ballroom of the casino. It was a beautiful sight with eight rows of eight tables in the center of the room. Set further back surrounding the tables, was the audience section, which was similar to the tiered seating in a movie theater.

Behind that was a bar and some tables where customers could sit and order dinner if they desired.

"Wow, this place is nuts," said Archie. "We've got about a half-hour before the tournament begins. I'm gonna head over and check in with the judges, but first I'm gonna grab a beer."

"Hey Arch, you might want to take it easy on the beer. You've got a ways to go tonight. This thing is scheduled for several hours."

"I know," said Archie. "I'll take it easy. I just want to take the edge off. You know."

"Yeah, I know," said Jim. "I know you… like for the past forty-five years."

Jimmy walked over and grabbed a program from one of the young ladies that was handing them out.

He started to read about the names given to the individual rounds and the rules, which determined the way each round would be played:

The Draughts tournament will feature several different variations on the game, with five rounds of elimination featuring a different type of world play. The tournament starts with 64 registered players. Each game has set rules with no draws allowed.

The person with no pieces, or a piece that is locked due to being unable to move, is the loser. There is a fifteen-minute break between each round.

At the end of the elimination rounds, there will be two players remaining for the final round.

An individual piece is called a man, and a double stacked piece is called a king.

That much Jimmy knew.

The first round will feature the traditional American or English Draughts, where the first move is by black and allowing no flying kings or allowing any captures by moving backwards.

Again, Jimmy was familiar with this version, as he had played it a few times with his grandpa.
He read on...

The second round will be played with the Italian version, where individual men cannot jump kings.

The third round will be played in "Shashki" or the Russian version of checkers, which allows a man that enters the king's row during a jump, to continue to jump backwards, jumping backwards as a king, and not as a man.

The fourth round will be played with the Canadian version of the game, and will feature a ten by ten square board, versus the standard eight by eight square board.

The fifth round will be played between the final 4 players, with only two contestants to move on to the final game. This will be a repeat version of English Draughts, with the added feature that kings may move and attack in any of the eight directions.

The sixth and final round will feature the final two contestants and will be played with the game board comprised of the ten by ten square variation in alternating dark and light colors, of which only the fifty dark squares are used. Each player will have twenty pieces, light for one player and dark for the other, at opposite sides of the board.

All moves and captures are made diagonally. All references to squares refer to the dark squares only. Pieces can also capture backward (not only forward), the long-range moving and capturing capability of kings (known as flying), and the requirement that the maximum number of men be captured whenever a player has capturing options.

In the starting position, the pieces are placed on the first four rows closest to the players. This leaves two central rows empty. White moves first. Enemy pieces can and must be captured by jumping over the enemy piece, two squares forward or backward to an unoccupied square immediately beyond. If a jump is possible it must be done, even if doing so incurs a disadvantage.

Multiple successive jumps forward or backward in a single turn can and must be made if after each jump there is an unoccupied square immediately beyond the enemy piece. It is compulsory to jump over as many pieces as possible. One must play with the piece that can make the maximum number of captures.

As with any of the aforementioned games, a player's turn ends when he takes his finger off the playing piece. A player may take back the move and remove, as long as he has not removed his finger from the piece.

Once a player makes his or her move, they will record that move on their player's record sheet. Judges hold the right to disqualify any player making an unauthorized move in the specific variation of Draughts being played.

"Wow," Jimmy thought. "This is way more complicated than I ever imagined." His appreciation for Archie grew.

Archie smiled at Jim as he turned and walked up to the bar. He noticed a gentleman a few stools down who looked an awful lot like Marlon Tinsdale, the world-class checkers champion from England. He was wearing a sharp-looking blue blazer with an ivory colored ascot. Archie walked over and introduced himself.

"Uh, hi. Aren't you Marlon Tinsdale, from England?"

"Why, yes old man. Indeed I am. And you are?"

Marlon looked Archie up and down, clearly not impressed with his checkered shirt and white loafers.

"I'm Archie Reynolds, from Philly. Well, originally from Poughkeepsie, New York. Nice to meet ya'."

The two shook hands and Marlon glanced down at Archie's wrapped up finger.

"My God, Man. What happened to your hand?"

"Oh, Just a sports related injury, you could say. I got hit with a baseball and it busted my finger. Won't stop me from checkers, though."

"We refer to the game as Draughts," said Marlon in a slightly snobbish air.

"Oh, yeah. Well, sure. Draughts it is. I mean, that is the proper name, right? Speaking of draughts, would you like a beer? My treat. I'm gonna have a Schlitz myself."

"Macallan and water for me, lad," said Marlon.

The bartender poured the drinks and brought Archie the tab, which made his eyes bulge when he saw the price of the scotch.

"Must be some good stuff," he said quietly under his breath, forking over some dough to the bartender.

He turned to Marlon and raised his glass. "Cheers, Marlon."

"Yes, cheers old man," said Marlon, taking a sip of his scotch.

"I don't imagine the competition will be as fierce as the Queen's finals I won last year. But one must prepare for anything, I suppose."

"Yeah, I suppose," said Archie, taking a gulp of his Schlitz and wiping the foam from his upper lip with his cardigan sleeve. "You do this as a full time job?"

"No, I delve in real estate mostly. But I do enjoy traveling to all the best tournaments. Sort of a hobby, you could say."

"Kind of a hobby for me, too," said Archie. "Although I haven't faced any real competition in quite a while."

"Really? So how many tournaments have you won in the states?"

"Well, I uh... I won the Poughkeepsie, New York finals, uh... back in 1938."

"Poughkeepsie, hmmm... I've never heard of that one. Any more recent tournaments?"

"Well, uh no. Traveling really wasn't in the cards for me. I got married in my early twenties and went into the service. When I got back home, I decided to open up a store in downtown Philly. But I've kept up with the game. I play mostly every afternoon, and I still get my Wood's Checker Player magazines in the mail," Archie said proudly.

"Right," said Marlon, taking another sip of scotch and looking at his gold Rolex.

"Well, it's been a fun chat old man, but I must be meeting a few people before the match starts."

"Good luck to you," said Archie. "Who knows, maybe we'll meet during one of the matches."

"Right. Best of luck, old man," said Marlon, who smiled half-heartedly and walked away.

"Nice guy, that Marlon," said Archie to himself, who finished his Schlitz and walked over to the judges table to check in.

By the time Jim, Terri and Jimmy got to their seats, the tournament was about to start. The announcer for the evening gave a brief description of the first round and announced that the match was to now begin.

Archie was seated at one of the tables. Across from him sat a large man dressed in a brown tweed suit. He looked to be about thirty-five years of age and reminded Archie of one of his high school professors. The two shook hands and wished each other good luck. Archie had chosen black, and made his first move.

It was a side piece that he slid in and forward. His trademark move to start a game, he always preferred to start at the sides and move in, preferably forming an attack wedge.

His opponent countered by moving one of his pieces forward to stop Archie from advancing without giving up a jump.

This continued until Archie's opponent could only respond by moving one of his men into the middle zone.

At that point Archie jumped and continued to slide from the back-forward leaving his opponent in the same predicament again and again.

After ten minutes, Archie had taken most of his opponent's pieces, and his opponent yielded play. He stood and shook Archie's hand.

One of the judges who was assigned to overlook their board, pointed toward Archie and confirmed him the winner of his match in round one.

Jim stood up and applauded, and Terri gave Jimmy a hug.

One by one, each table was awarded a victor and after a ten-minute break, the next match began.

Round two began with Archie's opponent moving first. Archie had hardly ever played opposing red. He knew he was slightly superstitious, but he didn't care. He felt as if black was his victory color. He needed to push that from his mind. He was assigned red, and that was that.
His opponent for this round looked to be the same age as Archie. He looked at Archie over the top of his glasses and held a blank expression

on his bearded face. Perhaps not to be rude, but maybe it was his way of achieving deep concentration.

Deep concentration or not, after fifteen minutes, Archie had won two kings and was starting to implement them into the next phase of his game plan. His opponent had only one king, but had more pieces in play on the board. It had cost Archie a few men in order to get that second king, now in the back row.

But in the Italian version, men cannot jump kings, so Archie felt even though he was outnumbered, he still had an advantage. Archie knew that he could let those kings sit for now, safe in the back row. Now he could move his remaining men forward to get that third king. his opponent would have no choice but to move one of his back men forward on the board. When the time was right, Archie ceased the movement forward and used one of his back kings to capitalize on the gap that remained. The first time, Archie took one man. The second time, his opponent had left two aligning gaps and Archie used one of his kings in a "flying" move, which jumped forward and then sideways to take two of his opponent's black pieces.

Now Archie had the advantage going forward. His opponent no longer outnumbered him and was down one king, to Archie's two.

Archie moved his kings forward and in for the kill. His confidence was high, as he hadn't remembered ever being dominant in a game while using red.

As his opponent moved up to address Archie's men, which were slowly advancing toward the back row, Archie would pick them off with one of his two kings.

It was over. He had his opponent's last two pieces pinned against the side of the board with nowhere to move. In a familiar gesture, his opponent stood and shook Archie's hand, and Archie was declared the winner.

Once again, cheers rang out from a small section of of the crowd.

When all tables had completed the second round, a fifteen-minute break was declared and Archie stood up and walked toward his friends.

Jim was beaming as he walked up to Archie and congratulated him on winning his first two rounds.

"Great job, champ. You got these guys on the ropes. Just keep your left up and go for the head."

"Haa. Funny, coach. It only gets tougher from here. We play the Russian version next."

"Then I say, good luck comrade," said Jim.

Before the next round started, Archie chose black, which was a random selection made by choosing a piece from an undisclosed box. The judge hit the timer at their table to start play, and Archie was ready for his opening move.

His opponent was a woman in her late fifties from California. She had a piercing gaze, which caught Archie off guard a bit, as he was used to players staring at the board and not him.

When it was her turn she tended to mirror Archie on every move. Another thing he wasn't used to. So he decided to do something risky. He make a move that he wouldn't normally do, which left his piece unguarded from a follow-up jump. She followed suit.

"Interesting," he thought. He then planned to trap her in a double jump by thinking a few moves ahead. Sure enough she mirrored his move. But when Archie went to set up the second of the moves in his plan, she switched strategies and turned the tables on him, by jumping one of his men.

"Okay, deal's off," he said to himself. He had read about this type of player at his time in the library. They use the opponent's knowledge to piggy back their moves until they found an opening.

Archie decided to ignore her completely. He no longer looked up to see if she was watching him. He decided to focus purely on the board and to pretend he was playing Jim, back on the green in Philly.

It started to work. He was able to take one of her men toward the back of the board and double-jump backwards in the same move. Once he had that king, things started to go his way. The match ended with Archie gaining three kings to her one. He hit the timer clock to mark his last move, and as a result, took her last king.

The game was over, as her remaining pieces were border locked. As they shook hands, she congratulated him on his play and offered to buy him a drink.

"My name's Angela," she said. "Sorry for the staring. It's part of my game plan. Trying to get my opponent to focus on me and not the board has worked in the past."

"An interesting strategy. It had me for a while," said Archie.

Angela ordered a glass of wine and Archie got his standard beer. They traded phone numbers to keep in touch, which was something of a surprise to him, as he wasn't used to women asking for that. But it seemed a good way to keep in touch with a fellow aficionado of the game. Jim and Terri waved from a distance, and Jimmy gave Archie the thumbs up to approve of his company.

As Archie finished his beer and went back to the game floor for the next round, he looked across the floor to see Marlon Tinsdale still in the game. A part of him had wished he would have been eliminated by now, but obviously, he was a top contender.

The fourth round was to be the Canadian version of the game and would use a ten by ten square board. Archie had again drawn black. His opponent was a tall man, who looked to be from the west, as he wore a large cowboy hat, boots and a vest. He shook Archie's hand and said "Hi, I'm Earl," in a deep voice with a southwestern drawl.

"Archie Reynolds," he replied. "Good luck to you."

Archie's first move was the same as his game plan from the first round. Keeping conservatively to the side pieces and watching for an opening. No flying kings would be allowed, which again meant that kings could move in any direction, but only one space at a time, unless double-jumping.

Earl was a savvy player, as his strategy was aggressive in nature. He lost a piece here and there to Archie, but also captured a few of Archie's by double-jumping Archie's pieces when one of his risky moves worked. Five minutes into the match, they were tied with two kings each and four men each remaining on the board.

Archie then set up Earl beautifully, as he knew Earl would quickly want another king to put the board in his advantage, so Archie lured him in, knowing that his men were just as powerful as a king if double-jumping. When Earl made a move to get his next king by jumping one of Archie's men. Archie's nearby man double-jumped Earl and took a king as well as another red man.

Now Archie was up by one man, and focused on using the path he had just created on the right side, to get his next man into the back row. He used a king as an escort, and Earl could do nothing to stop him. A few minutes later, Archie had three kings to Earl's two, plus the extra man. Earl then made an all-out race for the back row, but Archie beat him there again and was up another king.

The match ended with Earl making a nice jump on Archie's king, but Archie quickly did the same and stayed two pieces up for the remainder of the game.

Earl nodded his head in compliance to Archie's strategy and shook his hand.

"Thanks, Archie," he said. "That was one fine game."

The next break was to be twenty minutes, and Archie could see that Marlon had once again defeated his opponent.

Jim, Terri and Jimmy were ecstatic at Archie's success. Archie was modest and admitted that the last round was pretty difficult, but the one to come would really test his knowledge. It would be the English Draughts version on the standard eight by eight board, but kings could fly across open squares to make a capture in any of the eight directions, as long as the square opposite the piece was open for the jump.

As Archie sat down at his table, he was surprised to see Marlon sit down opposite him.
"Well, well," said Marlon, "We meet again."

"Right back at ya. I was hoping we would meet in the final," replied Archie, which was an outright fib, as Archie had hoped that Marlon would have been eliminated by now.

The two shook hands and Marlon proceeded to draw his piece. It was black.

"Damn," Archie thought to himself. "Just gonna have to do it. Red it is. Just gonna have to do it for Jimmy."

Marlon opened from the side of the board, just as Archie had done earlier. Archie decided to take a page from Angela's book and mirrored Marlon's move.

When Marlon moved another man, Archie did the same. Marlon looked up only to see Archie staring back. Archie held his gaze straight at Marlon. He could see him growing slightly frustrated with his mirroring move strategy. Then, Archie abandoned the move and made an opening for Marlon, which he had to jump. There was no choice for him, as the rules stated. Marlon made the jump and Archie then made a double jump which landed in the back row for a king.

Marlon's next move was to slide one of his pieces forward diagonally to block Archie's flying king from finding an open path. This allowed for Archie to slide another man further toward the back row.

Eventually Marlon had to make a move for the back, which opened a jump for Archie. But Marlon counter jumped him.

Archie then moved his back side piece into the back row for his second king. Marlon then did the same for his first king. But Archie now had an open path and flew his king straight ahead and made a double jump on two of Marlon's men.

Archie would only lose two more men before he had complete control of the board. Marlon's final move was to try and back up one of his remaining men, but Archie's flying king took it out. It was a move that sacrificed one of his kings, but it didn't matter, with Archie up two pieces and the advantage of an extra king, he was able to lock Marlon's remaining two pieces and the match was over.

Marlon was shocked at his defeat. But nonetheless, he offered Archie his hand and nodded his head once in defeat.

Jim jumped clear out of his chair and shouted, "Way to go, Arch!!" which was met with a couple of stares in his direction for the sheer volume of his outburst.

The other match had already been decided, and Archie could see it was what looked to be a young teenager who remained victorious.

One of the judges called a thirty-minute break before the sixth and final match was to begin.

Archie joined Jim and his family at a side table where they all gave Archie words of encouragement. Jimmy gave Archie a hug and Terri explained how she was so impressed to see Archie in the final match. Even Jim admitted that it was amazing how he defeated Marlon.

Archie ordered a Schlitz and took a sip from the lager. He felt relaxed as he watched the small bubbles continually float up to the surface. Looking over, he could see the young man who was to be his opponent, joined by his parents, who were equally happy, congratulating him on his win.

As Archie picked up the glass to take another sip, he suddenly stopped and put the glass back on the table. He didn't feel the need to finish it. He had never felt that way before, but he decided that he didn't need the beer to feel relaxed. He was among the closest thing to family that he had in his life and he was going to enjoy the moment. He looked over at Jimmy, who was thumb wrestling with Jim. Terri looked on and laughed as Jimmy struggled to pin Jim's large thumb.

"I'll play the winner," said Terri, whose gaze was just locked on Jimmy. Archie could see the love in her eyes as she watched Jim give way so Jimmy could pin his thumb.

Archie captured the moment with his Polaroid and then got ready for his upcoming match.

He was confident as he approached the table. When he drew black, he felt better, still.

The judge then introduced both of the finalists.

"Archie Reynolds, from Philadelphia, Pennsylvania and Tim Barrows, from Franklin, Kentucky."

Archie shook Tim's hand and wished him good luck, and Tim did the same for Archie. The judge started the timer and the match began. Each player would have sixty seconds to make each of their moves.

The board was once again the larger ten by ten squares. Each player would have twenty pieces. Individual pieces could now capture backward as well as forward, with all kings being able to fly and make multiple captures. If a player was offered a jump, they had to make it.

Archie decided to create a forward wedge this time, by starting from the center of the board and backing each move by filling in from behind. The strategy required that he pull his strength toward either the left or right side of the board to create the wedge. He chose left.

Tim decided to ignore the wedge at first and move his pieces from the side toward the inner part of the board and likewise, fill in from behind. It was on Archie's seventh move that Tim made his first jump. Archie had set him up and Tim had to make the jump.

But when Archie returned the jump to capture one of Tim's pieces, Tim double jumped him in return.

Archie couldn't believe it. Tim had allowed it to happen. He could clearly see three moves ahead.

Archie had always patted himself on the back for being able to see three moves ahead as well, but that had always been his limit, or maybe just all he had ever needed.

Archie regrouped his thoughts. He was only down nineteen pieces to seventeen. It was far from over. He could do this.

Archie started to rebuild his wedge, but the young man from Kentucky kept working his pieces in perpendicular to Archie's.

Once again the young man fell into one of Archie's traps, only to bounce back on a counter move, which Archie had not seen.

Halfway through the match, Archie was down twelve pieces to Tim's fifteen. There was a clear avenue on the right side for Tim to reach the back row, and although Archie knew his pieces could go backwards as well as forwards, to race after him would be fruitless.

Archie stared at the clock, which no longer felt like his friend. Twenty seconds went by. Thirty, then forty. He need to make a move. Archie decided to continue down the left side and was close to gaining a king when Tim reached the back row first and crowned his piece.

Archie then pushed his piece into the back row and gained his first king, but in doing so, he left open a jump for Tim.

The young man wasn't sure if it was a baited move, as he studied the board. But according to the rules, he had to make the jump and in doing so, captured another of Archie's men.

As Archie slid another piece closer to the back row, Tim set up his next trap. He slid a piece diagonal toward Archie, which he had no choice but to jump. There was no return jump initially.

"Had the kid messed up?" Archie thought. He studied the board and then quickly realized it was a sacrificial move. It allowed Tim to flow another piece into the back row and to be crowned, only this time there was a successive jump available and Tim's king instantly went backwards diagonally, flying to another of Archie's men and then another.

It was clear to Archie now that Tim could see four moves ahead. Archie was now down a king and several men. "Anything could happen," he thought. He just needed another king.

But as the game went on, several more pieces fell to Tim's flying kings and Archie just couldn't capitalize on any multiple jumps.

In the end, Archie ended up with two kings, unable to move due to being locked by Tim's remaining six pieces, four of them being kings. It was over. Tim had won.

"It couldn't be," Archie thought. "It wasn't supposed to end this way."

He just stared at the board. But it wasn't changing. He had lost and the only remaining thing to do was to congratulate the young man from Kentucky. Archie stood up across from Tim and offered him his hand.

"You played an amazing game," said Archie.

"And you were a worthy opponent," said Tim. "Good luck to you."

Archie looked over at the crowd, where Jim, Terri and Jimmy were sitting. Their faces had clearly changed from a celebratory cheer, to supportive smiles because they didn't want him to feel badly. He knew that look, and although it wasn't the look he wanted, it was what family does when they love you and support you.

The head judge announced Tim as the winner and presented him with a large check for fifteen thousand dollars. Tim's family cheered and his mom jumped up and down. Archie was glad they were happy.

The judge also awarded Archie a check for five hundred dollars, for coming in second place in the tournament. Jim, Terri and Jimmy clapped and they all gave Archie a hug as he returned to them.

"Well, it looks as though I won enough dough to buy back the Bel Air," said Archie is a somber tone. He almost started to cry as he looked his good friend in the eyes.

Archie didn't have the immediate courage to look over at Jimmy and Terri. "I'll be right back," he said, as he walked head down across the room and over to the restrooms.

"Is he alright?" asked Jimmy.

"He's okay," said Jim. "Just a little deflated right now. If I know Archie, he'll bounce back."

Archie walked back and handed the signed check over to Jim.

"I'm sorry, pal. I really am."

"You did your best," said Terri. "It's all we could have asked for."

"Did I? Somehow I don't think so," said Archie.

"Mr. Reynolds, you came in second place. You did great. Please don't feel bad," said Jimmy.

"Thanks, kid," said Archie. "I just need to be alone for a bit. Gonna take a walk. I'll see you guys a bit later."

Outside, Archie let out a long, deep sigh. He tried to look up at the stars, but there was too much light pollution. At least the cool night air was less stale than the casino hall.

Archie walked past the bright lights of the towering casinos and street signs, hands in his pockets and head held low. He had let his best friend down and he felt awful about it. It was his one chance to shine, to help Jimmy and Terri, and he blew it. It was all right there in front of him and he just couldn't seem to make the right moves. He wished so bad he could do it over again, but that's not how life is. You make your moves and you live with the results.

He had even pictured Jimmy's smiling face when he would have received the winning trophy and check. Instead, it went to the young man from Franklin, Kentucky.

"At least his family would be proud," he said to himself.

For almost all of his life he had known Jim. The friend that stuck with him through thick and thin... and Jimmy... man, how he loved that kid.

Tears ran down his cheeks and he pulled out his hanky to blow his nose. There had to be another way.

He walked for what felt like miles, past many of the casinos, fancy restaurants and bars. Feeling a bit weak and hungry, he took out his wallet and looked inside. Eight dollars. Maybe enough to grab a bite and take a cab back to the motel.

He hadn't eaten in the last five hours. He saw a small pizza restaurant across the street and crossed over the busy road.

"Luigi's," it said on the brightly lit sign. The sign inside said seat yourself, so he sat down in a booth on one of the firm red upholstered benches. The restaurant looked fairly busy for this time at night.

A small man walked up and welcomed him.

"Hello Paisan, welcome. Someone will be right over."

Archie nodded in response and looked at the menu by the napkin dispenser. He saw they offered pizza by the slice.

"A few slices of pepperoni should do the trick," he thought.

A couple minutes later a woman came back to take his order. She placed a basket with some breadsticks in front of him.

"Thank you," said Archie. "I'll have two slices of pepperoni please and a Schl..." He was about to say Schlitz, but stopped himself. "I'll have a Coke, please."

The woman wrote his order, smiled and walked back to the kitchen. As Archie looked around, he could tell the place was very clean and in great condition. The benches looked spotless and the walls looked newly papered. There were scenes of Italian landscapes with vineyards and sunsets. There were a couple of Chianti bottles on a shelf, each one wrapped in a traditional basket weave. It was welcoming. He started to feel a bit better.

The woman came back and brought his Coke with a straw and his two warm pepperoni slices. Her smile was warm and glowing.

"Enjoy. Mangia," she said with a smile before walking back to the kitchen.

The two pizza slices went down fast. As Archie drank the rest of his soda, he was cognizant of the bottom of the glass, and didn't want to make the slurping sound that would always get on Jim's nerves.

He kept thinking of Jim, Terri and Jimmy. They might be worried. He probably should get back to the motel.

As he walked to the counter to pay, the woman asked if everything was satisfactory.

"It was great," he answered. "Best pizza I've had in a long time. Reminds me of a place back home in Philadelphia."

"Grazie. Thank you so much. We have only been open for a few weeks. My husband and I used to have a much smaller place further outside of town, but we decided to expand for the first time."

"Well, I wish you the best of luck," said Archie.

As he walked back down the brightly lit street, Archie took out his pipe, tamped the tobacco inside the bowl slightly and lit it up. The sweet smell of Captain Black filled the air around him and he thought about how much he enjoyed the pizza restaurant. He thought of the woman's smiling face and how he hoped they would be successful. They seemed to be doing fine. There were so many smiling happy faces inside, enjoying each other's company and the smells and tastes of the wonderful food.

Soon, he thought, this would be a distant memory and he'd be back home in his store on Main Street. His quiet, lonely store. He took another puff of his pipe and started thinking. The more he thought about the good food and smiles, the more he smiled and the faster he puffed. He was like a small locomotive starting off down a track.

The wheels started spinning slowly, then faster. Puff... puff. Archie quickened his pace and his head lifted ever so slightly upward, puff...puff...puff.

Archie had an idea, a wonderful idea.

Chapter XXIV

It was several hours later when Archie walked into the motel room. The sun had just started to come up. He quietly walked past Jimmy and Jim, who were still asleep in their double bed.

Archie quietly took off his blazer and white loafers, and was about to lie down when he saw something on his pillow. It was a small paper note, written in crayon. The same crayons from a familiar Big Boy restaurant.

It read:

Dear Archie,

Thank you so much for trying your best in the checkers game.
I know you tried very hard and Gramps and I love you very much.

-Jimmy.

P.S. I hope your smashed finger is feeling better.

For the second time in one night, a tear ran down Archie's face. He looked over at the sweet kid lying next to his grandpa.

"Don't you worry, kid," Archie whispered. "I'm here for you."

Archie's head hit the pillow and he was out like a light.

The following morning, Archie woke to find the motel room empty. It looked like the guys had showered and dressed, and left Archie to his slumber.

The clock on the nightstand read eleven a.m.

"Holy cow," said Archie, as he quickly sat up. "I really slept late."

And with that, he quickly showered. As he opened the front door, wearing only his bath towel, he peeked outside. He figured the guys had gone out to get breakfast, and then maybe over to the pawn shop to reclaim the Bel Air.

Archie dressed and wrote a note saying he'd be back soon, and walked down the road at a sharp pace, like a man with a mission.

It was a few hours later when Archie arrived back at the motel. He smiled, as he could see that the Bel Air was back, and most likely the guys too.

He knocked on the front door and was greeted by Jim. "Hey, pal. Good to see you! You were sleeping like a log and Jimmy and I were hungry, so we went for a bite to eat. You must have gotten in super late."

"Yeah, I had some thinking to do."

"Everything alright?" asked Jim.

"More than alright," answered Archie, as he placed an envelope in Jim's large hand,

"What's this?" asked Jim.

"Just open it," said Archie.

Jim opened the envelope as his mouth hung open. He looked up at Archie for a second and then back at the envelope.

"You didn't like... rob a bank or anything?" Jim whispered softly so Jimmy couldn't hear.

"Heck, no. Go ahead and count it."

Jim thumbed through the thick stack of bills and counted fifteen thousand dollars in total.

"It's for Terri," said Archie. "I decided to finally sell the store back home."

"You what??? You sold your antique shop?"

"Old man Bertolini has been after me for years, so he could expand and upgrade his restaurant. So, I made a deal and he wired me the money this morning. He buys the shop and then keeps me on the payroll as head waiter."

"You, head waiter?"

"Yeah, I like the idea. I'll have to get some black loafers of course, but I like the idea. Plus, get this... I get free eats."

Jim grabbed Archie and gave him one of his patented bear hugs, which lifted Archie off the ground and almost clear out of his loafers.

"I can't believe you. You're the best friend a guy ever had," said Jim. "I don't know how to thank you."

"You and Jimmy already have," said Archie. "Okay. I need to breathe now."

Jim chuckled as he lowered Archie, releasing his bear hug.

"Jimmy," shouted Jim. "Everything is going to be alright!"

Chapter XXV

It was seven a.m on a clear, sunny day, when the Nassau blue, '57 Bel Air pulled up to the Cup-O-Joe. Only one occupant was in the car. He stared up at the large metal sign, adorned with the neon bars, that when lit up, could be seen for miles in the distance at night. Up close, he could see the bird droppings, the multitude of metal rivets and areas of where the paint had been worn clean from sun, wind and sand.

He liked the name of the diner, but not the skunk that owned it. Cup-o-Joe was what they called coffee back when he served his country. What had started out as an abbreviation for Mocha-Java, or "Jamoke", had become a name for the common man's drink and every man, every "Joe" that served in order to protect the common man, and ultimately, everything they held dear. The scum that owned this place, hadn't earned the right to name it with those specific words, even if Rick's last name really was Coffee.

The driver's door made its usual metallic creak as big Jim got out.

He zipped his windbreaker up halfway and then took his tweed cap off, ran his fingers straight back through his thinning grey hair and placed it back on, with just the right amount of tilt.

Grabbing a small leather satchel off the passenger seat, he closed the door on the '57 and walked inside. He could tell they had just opened, as two waitresses in the place were still wiping down the tables and putting out the morning's placemats. He tipped his cap to the lady he remembered from his previous visit.

"Good morning, Michelle. Your boss in yet?"

"Yes, he's back in his office. I can let him know you want to see him. You're Terri's friend, Jim, right?"

"Yup. But that's okay, Michelle, I know where the office is... and he'll see me."

Jim walked past the front counter and the restrooms and around the corner to where Rick's office was. The door was closed. Off to the side on the wall, was the stupid stuffed jackalope. He almost felt sorry for the dumb animal. If it wasn't bad enough for the jackrabbit to have been killed and stuffed, some idiot decided to place antlers on his head so he could spend the rest of eternity as some novelty, mounted on a wall just past the restrooms.

Across from Rick's office was another room. The door was ajar and Jim looked inside. A small table with a lamp, a mirror on the wall, and a cot with a pillow and blanket were the only items in the room. A single shower stall was off to one side.

A small, sliding window only allowed in a few rays of sunshine to cast their glow on the dismal place. He thought of Terri and how lonely she must have been these past years, to sleep in this place and feel like she had nowhere else to go.

Jim turned back toward Rick's office and knocked on the door with the first two knuckles of his large hand. He could hear someone inside shuffling around, then what sounded like a tipped over bottle.

With no answer, he knocked once again, only this time a voice shouted back from within.

"What the hell do you want Michelle? Just open up for business, will ya? I'll be out later."

Jim twisted the door knob and found it wasn't locked. Inside was Rick Coffee, sitting at his desk. There was a small unmade cot in the corner, and Rick looked like he had slept in his clothes. Next to many strewn papers on the desk was a shot glass and a bottle of Jim Beam, which was empty and turned on its side.

"I made the trip here today just for you, Rick. Here, this is for you. It's from Terri."

Jim unceremoniously tossed the small leather satchel onto the desk in front of Rick. Rick looked up at Jim, puzzled and then unzipped it and looked inside. His eyes widened as he pulled several stacks of bills from the bag and proceeded to thumb through it.

"It's all there," said Jim. "Everything she owed you. Fourteen thousand and eighty-two dollars. Terri's square with you now and doesn't want to see your face again. And just in case you were curious, those were her exact words."

Untrustingly, Rick continued to thumb through the bills. Jim interrupted him by slipping his hand under his windbreaker and pulling out a piece of paper, which he unfolded and slammed down on the desk, directly in from of Rick.

"Just one last thing. Sign and date this, Ricky boy."

"What the hell is this?" shouted Rick.

"It's a receipt, stating that you've been paid what Terri owed you. Clean break. Now sign it."

"Look, old man, I don't have to sign anything!" shouted Rick. "My numbers could have been off. She might owe me hundreds or maybe thousands more for all I know. I'll need to go through my books."

Without hesitation, Jim reached across the desk with his large hands and grabbed Rick Coffee by the front of his shirt and lifted him fully out of his chair. The tips of his toes were barely touching the floor.

Suddenly, Rick looked scared. It was a face Jim had seen many times in his life, from the inside of a ring at the Spectrum, to the hellish beaches of Guam.

Holding Rick firmly with his left hand, Jim popped out his front false teeth with his right hand and held them closely in front of Rick's face for a good second, then popped them back in.

"I don't give a rat's ass who you're connected to. You either sign and date that goddamn receipt right now, or I'm gonna personally see to it, you get a set of these!"

Rick stared at the large fist held back in front of him, and then at the scowl on Jim's face.

"Ok... I'll sign."

Jim released him and Rick fell back into his chair. He promptly signed and dated the receipt.

Taking the the paper back, Jim glanced at the writing and quickly compared it to a signature that was on his cluttered desk. It was correct.

"I'd like to say it was nice doing business with you Rick, but it wasn't. I don't ever want to see your face again, either."

With that, Jim slammed the door on his way out of Rick's office.

The cheap, thin trailer walls shook like the roll of thunder, and the jackalope fell off his perch and onto the floor. Jim looked down at the silly thing as he walked past. He could swear it was smiling.

Chapter XXVI

The sun was shining brightly down on the '57 Bel Air, as its driver and three passengers enjoyed the warmth on their faces.

'Ol' Blue Eyes' was singing on the radio and Archie's loafers were tapping gently to the beat. His mind was filled with excitement at the thought of his new job as head waiter, as he no longer felt the weight on his shoulders of having to run a business for the next decade. He gently pulled the small piece of paper from his shirt pocket and smiled as he once again read Angela's phone number.

Jim, who was very much enjoying his new clean and clear windshield, glanced back for a second and smiled when he saw Jimmy laying across the bench with his head on Terri's lap, relaxing and staring up at the morning sky.

Terri ran her fingers through Jimmy's hair. It fondly reminded her of a long time ago when she used to do the same thing for Danny.

Jimmy's hair had gotten lighter over the past few weeks in the sun. Terri noticed some of the red highlights that she sometimes would get, too. A new life awaited her back in Philly, and although she was planning to finish some of the songs she had going through her head, she was most especially looking forward to having "Mom" be the most important title she would ever hold, for the rest of her life.

Smiling and looking up at the white puffy clouds in the bright blue sky, was a content ten-year-old. Everything just seemed to be right. There were no worries of the upcoming fifth grade year. No thoughts of the paper route back home, or whether Mike Savoy and Sam had done a good job. There was just contentment. Here, in this very moment he honestly and truly felt loved.

He wondered if his dad could see them now. He remembered how Gramps would often say that they'd all be together again, someday.

At the time, he had guessed Gramps meant heaven, but he wasn't quite sure what or where heaven was. Maybe it was a picture of them together, embracing each other, like long lost family or friends would often do upon reuniting.

He could see his father, putting on the stereo and starting to dance. The vision became clearer.

His dad reaching out and gently taking his mom's hands in his. Pulling her close as Elvis played on the stereo. The soft song he loved so much, about falling in love.

There, in that magical place somewhere in the future, they danced and held each other close, as if they had never parted. For those were the birthday wishes of a ten-year-old boy.

Also from Christopher Karam:

Signs of Life
Signs of Courage
Signs of Redemption

Made in the USA
Middletown, DE
27 September 2020